High Spirits

Malcolm Stewart

I wrote this book not only as a reminder and record of the key changes that took place in my young life, after joining Her Majesty's Royal Air Force. But also as a light hearted pick-me-up and possible training guide, for any young twenty year old down on their luck, or having a few problems as a result of their living environment. It can and does get better, but please bear-in-mind, around eighty per cent of this book is what not to do.

There is too many of the younger generation, that believe the older generation, never did anything wrong their whole lives. That is an impossible burden, for the younger generation to have to live up to and without a doubt, the older generation would love to reflect on some of the less intelligent pranks they pulled, before grey hair set in. This book will serve both purposes very well;

I often read the odd chapter of my own book, whenever I am slightly under par; this never fails to bring a smile back to my face. By having my book published, this would allow everybody else the same opportunities as I look forward to on a regular basis.

Malcolm Stewart

For information, address Comfort Publishing, 9450 Moss Plantation Avenue N.W., Suite 204, Concord, NC 28027. The views expressed in this book are not necessarily those of the publisher.

First printing

Book cover design
by Colin L. Kernes

ISBN:978-0-9821154-5-9
Published by Comfort Publishing, LLC
www.comfortpublishing.com

Printed in the United States of America

Chapter One-Caper One

It's the 21st of March, 1977. I'm on the train and heading for Lincoln. How I managed it, and it seems to be the
right train, I'm not really sure. This morning, my dad had
woken me two hours early with a bacon sandwich. The two
hours early didn't help much, but the bacon sandwich had
managed to curb my hangover a little. I'd had a couple of
beers with the lads as a going-away drink last night. Mum
had washed and ironed every piece of clothing I owned and
packed them into two large suitcases. As I left the house, I
stood on my doorstep, trembling.

My brother had told me when the letter arrived not to
be so cock-sure because anybody could make the odd mistake. My dad had said, "Don't screw this up, son. You know
you don't deserve this chance."

My mum put her arms around me and kissed my forehead. "Yes, you do deserve it," she'd said, "and I know you
won't mess it up."

I couldn't help thinking that maybe my dad and
brother had a point, and someone had made a mistake when
sending me my acceptance paperwork. I felt I was 10 years

old all over again, except for the hangover I had – there is no way that a 10-year-old would ever experience a hangover like this.

Today's the day, my life will change forever. Today's the day, I'm going to join the Royal Air Force (R.A.F.).

Two days ago, I decided to cut off all my golden locks for an R.A.F.-style haircut. I'd heard all the rumours that, as soon as you walk from the train, the R.A.F. barbers sheered you like sheep. That was not going to happen to me. I wasn't joining straight from school. I had street-cred, and I'm smarter than that.

Many years before, I had joined the Air Training Corps (A.T.C.) and I knew all the rules. So here I was – shoes shiny, trousers pressed and with an R.A.F. regulation haircut. Cost me 15 quid. There would be no need for the barber to even give me a second look. He would be able to see I was old-school; been there, done that, knew the rules.

This was a new beginning for me, and I had a head start. I was 19 years old and things hadn't gone that well so far. Now things were going to be different. I knew what I was getting myself into, unlike most of the 60 blokes I was about to become roommates with. My A.T.C. days will hold me in good stead, and now I was going to reap the benefits.

Travelling from Corby in Northamptonshire, it wasn't long before the train arrived at Lincoln station. As I walked onto the platform from the supposedly empty train, there were three or four other young lads who'd also walked off the same train with me. A good 10 to 12 were already on the platform. I could see almost immediately, I wasn't going to get lonely at R.A.F. Swinderby.

Maybe it was a joke. Maybe nobody was going to pick

us up, but just leave us there until there was only one person left. Maybe it was the R.A.F.'s way of saying, "How dare you ask to join the Air Force with your standard of education?" I still wasn't 100 percent sure the letter that the Air Force had sent me was actually meant for me.

That's it, it was a competition. Having moved to a strange environment, as I just had, it was amazing what rubbish was going through my head. There was nothing much for me to go back home to, except for my girlfriend, Tina, and Tina wasn't that important. The way things had been going for me, joining the R.A.F. was probably my last chance to make anything of myself. So, if it was a competition, it was one I could afford to win. I had nowhere else to go, and, besides, it had been a while since I had won anything.

I still haven't worked out to this day why the R.A.F. had accepted me. I'd always thought that you had to be intelligent to join the R.A.F. Mind you, I was only going to be a driver. You hardly needed to be Einstein for that.

Over the next hour or so, our numbers on the station platform swelled. Maybe 20 to 25 young men stood around in small groups, with very few words being spoken. That was the first time I'd spoken to Moss. Moss was his second name and, from now on, it would be his first as well. You have to keep things simple. I never did find out his first name. I later was to find out that he was the eldest in our group, at 22, with a wife and two small children – a strange time of life to start a new career in the R.A.F., if you ask me. But, then, we were all here for different reasons. I just hadn't worked mine out yet.

As we were talking, into the car park at the side of the platform, an R.A.F. bus turned up. I thought to myself, yet

3

another competition I was not going to win. Looking across to the car park, I could see a corporal standing in the bus doorway, smiling. He looked along the platform and, still smiling, said, "This is the transport for all the young men wishing to be conveyed to a career in Her Majesty's Royal Air Force."

To which about half of us said, "What did he say?"

After some 10 seconds of shuffling and mumbling, but heading in the general direction of the bus, the corporal stopped smiling and announced, in a clear and unmistakable voice, "Move yourselves, you horrible little bleeders."

For the next 12 weeks, I would never see that man smile again. For the next 12 weeks, we were all going to be called by our second name, if we were lucky, that is.

On the bus, I sat next to Moss and we talked about what had brought us to this point in our lives, where we needed to entrust the next 12 weeks to this loud, obnoxious, moronic, robotic corporal. The corporal then assured me, that's just what we had done, (he also mentioned his remarkably good hearing).

Moss turned to me and said, "I'll be alright when I get my name down for the Arctic skiing." He didn't smile. I waited for a smirk or even a grin – there was nothing. I think he really believed it! God help him.

After 30 minutes or so, we arrived at R.A.F. Swinderby. When the bus came to a stop, we were all marched from the bus (bearing in mind, about 80 percent didn't know how to walk properly, let alone march). Luckily enough, I had learned to march in the A.T.C.

We were led straight to our new accommodations, commonly known as our "Billet." Well, it was new in the

4

1940s. We all lined up outside with our bags and suitcases. Then we were told to leave our bags and, in an orderly fashion, walk through the door and pick out a bed space.

As I walked in, I could see one bed, one bed pack and one locker per bed space. As I remembered from my summer camp days in the A.T.C., the R.A.F. was still keeping it simple. At least I was wrong about the 60-man room. We were lucky; we had two rooms of 30. We were definitely privileged.

When picking out your bed space you had to remember that it was going to be home for the next 12 weeks, if you were one of the lucky ones. All the supposedly "hard" men had decided which beds they wanted and who they didn't want near them. I grabbed the nearest, with a window, and Moss took the one opposite. If he had grabbed the one next to me, I would have been slightly worried.

A young lad called Massey, in the next bed space to me, had decided he didn't want me next to him. With the exception of Moss, all the second names I use means I didn't become friendly enough to find out their first name. With an instant dislike for Massey, I never found out his first name.

This was my first day in the R.A.F., and it's all about pecking order. I looked, then smiled at Massey and said, "It's tough at the top. It must be even worse where you are." He then explained to me that he was from Manchester and was "hard as nails." I explained to him that I was from Glasgow and covered in skin, which is soft to the touch, and I was not moving anywhere. I walked towards the door as a grin slowly appeared on Massey's face. I smiled back. "Just going to get my bags. I am still not moving," I said. My first day in the Royal Air Force and already I was making new friends.

Although I had heard Massey was a hard man, he didn't look that big to me.

The following day we were all frogmarched straight to the barbers (being ex-A.T.C., I could do that as well). As we lined up, I thought to myself, "This barber wouldn't even ask me to sit down. My haircut was spot-on R.A.F. regulation. And it had cost me 15 quid!" But, for some strange reason, he asked me to sit down. Things were not going to plan and this was only my second day. Before the time my arse had hit the seat, he mowed the top of my hair off – and then my fringe – and before I got comfortable, I was a skinhead. Maybe I wasn't so smart after all, but then that's only one-nil to the R.A.F.. The game had only just started.

Swinderby was basically just brainwashing. Everything you did there was scheduled and you learned just what they wanted you to learn. There was no individualism and no using your own initiative, let alone any thinking outside the box. You were woken up at 5:30 in the morning and lights-out was at 9:30 in the evening (lights-out only means that you have to finish off your day's work in the dark). Your day was completely organized for you, with no gaps for you to think for yourself.

Basic training was all about the selection of Mr. Average, with very little time for anyone who could think for themselves. The corporal, who had now become our best friend (so he said), would now allow us to call him Staff. He would wake us up every morning, shouting, "Phone Mummy and Daddy. Tell them to bring lots of money. They can buy you out of the R.A.F., then they can take you home with them."

In the early weeks, there were blokes being sent home

6

daily. After five or six weeks that trend died off a little, but we were always reminded of when we were getting near Cease Training (C.T.). C.T. was simple – if you couldn't do something, like English or Math, (unless you could get someone to do your work for you), it was a case of good-bye and mind your arse out the door.

This system worked well; I honestly don't think there is any one person capable of passing basic training without help from somebody else. Because I had a little knowledge from my days in the A.T.C., it gave me something to barter with when I needed to complete an exam I knew nothing about. A lad called Simon knew all the academic stuff, whereas I could show him how to bull (shine) his shoes. Although we only tried that the once, the important part of bulling your shoes is to remove the impurities from the polish. The best way is to set fire to the polish, but only a little at a time, although Simon was convinced it would be quicker if he let it burn for longer. After letting it burn for much too long, he came to realize it was now near impossible to put out – and after he had jumped on his flaming polish tin without any success. He then decided to kick the burning polish tin into his open wardrobe and then close the doors behind it. He was now using the out-of-sight, out-of-mind theory. Unfortunately, that particular theory doesn't work in the real world. He then made things worse by blocking the doors to his wardrobe. With him standing right in the way, he made it impossible for anybody else to help. Eventually the corporal dragged him from in front of his wardrobe and put out the flames with a fire extinguisher. Shortly after that, Simon was C.T. I don't think he was going to be of any use to the R.A.F. in a stressful situation.

The corporal told us that wasn't the first time he'd had to put out a polish tin fire and I never told him whose idea it was to set fire to the polish in the first place. I think he had enough suspicions of his own and, besides, I had enough to worry about trying to replace Simon with someone to do my academic work.

During the latter part of my training, I had a lot of help from a lot of people. We were all competing as a flight and all flights were staggered-entry, with inter-flight competitions and rivalry with a rather large scoreboard. The general idea was for the flights that had been there longest to teach the newcomers, by way of humiliation, how to be a good airman. The rivalry also spilt over into battles between trainees in the same flight. One or two of those battles, I managed to get involved with myself. Generally, it was all good, clean competition, attributed to high spirits (we were going to hear a lot more about High Spirits).

One of our drill instructors was a very big lad who insisted he couldn't read or write. He also maintained that the only way he could keep us in check was to take us 'round the back of a hangar for a good kicking. This meant he could save himself from filling in loads of paperwork, which he would have to do if he went through the correct channels by charging us.

When the instructor explained this to us, one lad who had been managing quite well suddenly developed a problem with his marching. The drill instructor stopped us and, with a grin on his face, walked over to this lad and said, "Looks like we have our first customer." The instructor quick-time marched this lad around to the back of the hangar; four or five minutes later and the young lad returned on his own.

The drill instructor then returned some five minutes after him, holding a hanky over his nose.

He said, "As I said before, I don't charge anybody because I don't do paperwork. I'll take you for a good kicking." Then, while pointing to the young lad who had just returned from behind the hangar, said, "All except that little shit. He's getting charged."

Later, I talked to this young lad about it. He told me he was the Amateur Boxing Association (A.B.A.) North West champion. I felt a chill go down my spine, realizing that this was the second conversation I'd had with Massey.

Part of our training to enable us to march was to complete the Trent Walk – 27 miles long and over very rough ground. On the day we had to do it, we had rain, sleet, strong winds and very bright sunshine. We set up in groups of six in 15-minute intervals, but the weather caused havoc and within the first 10 miles, most of the groups had been reduced to two and three members.

Our group (Group C) was no different. We had been reduced to three and the weather was trying to deplete us even further. Group B had also been depleted down to three and, as we caught them up, we joined together to become one group. As we were marching, an R.A.F. ambulance stopped alongside of us. The medic told us to keep a lookout for a member of the group in front of us; they had rung in from a farmhouse somewhere in the area and reported an airman down with exhaustion, recovering somewhere in the hedgerow. We managed to push on through the weather, but couldn't find any signs of anybody in the hedgerow.

We had been the third group to set out on the route march, so we were astonished to find out we were the first

9

group to finish. As we got stuck into a loaf of bread and a bucket of soup each, we were aware of the extra activity in camp. There were R.A.F. and Army medical teams everywhere, all complaining about how dark it was getting. An officer approached us while we were gulping down our bread and soup.

"Who is team leader here," he asked.

"We don't actually have a team leader, Sir, but I talk more than anybody else...Sir," I replied.

"It sounds like you have a sense of humour, young man,"

"Yes, Sir," I replied.

"That could come in handy when I tell you that I want you to go back out with us."

The officer then carried on explaining. He told us that the young airman who had gone down with exhaustion still hadn't been found, and the airman who reported it had also not returned. He thought we may be able to pinpoint more accurately the hedgerow where he'd gone missing.

We finished of our soup and bread and then I had a little chuckle as I watched the rest of my group (Moss and Yjanic) trying to make it back to their feet. Thankfully, before I tried to stand, we were told the two lads had been found and we didn't have to go and rescue anybody. Later we were told that both airmen were C.T.; the one that had been laying in the hedgerow for not being fit, the other because while his mate lay freezing in the hedgerow covered with a green tarpaulin, he had been sitting, drinking tea and eating cake with the old lady whose phone he had used. The exhausted airman was found walking down the road with his green tarpaulin over his shoulder and told the ambulance crew that had found him that he had gotten bored waiting for them to rescue him. There was a lot of C.T. before we would get to the end of basic training.

The big day arrived. We had managed to survive and I had managed to avoid young Mr. Massey – quite an achievement, if I do say so myself. Today was our passing-out day – we had passed all our exams, finished all the assault courses and soaked up all that military brainwashing. It was early June and everybody was running around like headless chickens. With shiny shoes, best-pressed uniforms, and parents and girlfriends en route, it was going to be a good day. Everything was immaculate; if it didn't move, it was painted or polished. Most things were painted and polished, just to make sure.

They also gave us a gun to play with. Well, actually it was a rifle, but no bullets and with a large hole drilled through it, just to make sure we didn't shoot anybody. On the end of the barrel there was a bayonet with a sheath protector. As everything was being cleaned, I decided to remove the sheath and clean the blade.

My newfound friends, Moss, Danny, Paul and Yjanic, thought it might be a good idea to remove the blade and give it a good cleaning. (Removing a bayonet from a rifle can be quite tricky.) I was to find out later that cleaning the blade safely was a part of the training that Yjanic had missed.

The whole morning, in our own way, we had spent preparing for our Passing-out Parade. Everybody was nervous, but everybody knew what they had to do. We all started to line up outside our billet when I noticed Yjanic was not with us. I called to Moss, "Where is Yjanic?"

"He's in the medical centre. He'll meet us on the

parade ground," replied Moss with a big grin on his face. We marched down to the parade ground, taking advantage of the time to practice our drill movements for our passing-out parade.

The time had come – no going back now. We were all lined up in our best blues and, in the crowd, I could see my mum and Tina. During the last few years at home, things hadn't always gone to plan for me. I was going to get this right, and my mum was watching.

We all marched faultlessly and managed to complete our passing-out without any major embarrassing moments. I think it was the first time we had ever gone straight through without stopping; it had only taken us 12 weeks. At the end of the parade, the officer in charge addressed us all as airmen. We saluted him and then were dismissed. Again feeling like a 10-year-old, as I had 12 weeks earlier, I ran over to my mum and Tina.

My mum stood there grinning from ear to ear. "I've no idea how you manage it, but well done, son!" she exclaimed, then hugged and kissed me on the forehead. I also got a kiss from Tina, but it had been so long since I'd seen her, it really felt weird. Danny and Paul came over to where we stood. I don't think they had anybody to come and see them pass out.

"Have you seen Yjanic yet?" asked Danny.

"No I haven't. Where is he," I asked.

Neither Danny nor Paul replied; they just started to laugh. "What's up?" I said.

"Take your mum and girlfriend for a cup of tea," suggested Danny, and the two of them wandered off, still laughing.

Sometime later, I was to find out that when they were

cleaning their bayonets, Yjanic had struggled to take the bayonet from the rifle. Unfortunately, when he did manage it, he had already removed the protective sheath, then proceeded to stick the bayonet through his top lip and removed one of his front teeth. He didn't get to the parade, but he did serve tea and coffee to the audience, including his mum and dad, who had made a trip of several hundred miles to see their son pass out. I heard he lost a fair bit of blood and nearly had a passing-out of his own.

Maybe it had something to do with the intense workload or the level of fitness of our group, but when it came to leaving Swinderby, there could only have been 20 to 25 out of 60 airmen to complete the basic training course. One of the lads from another group had his own incentive to keep up with his exams. In the third week of our training (our first weekend off camp), he had met a girl who had been working as a barmaid at a pub called the Halfway House. He would leave camp after midnight and return before the 5:30 roll call, two or three times a week. I am not sure how much basic training he had achieved, but I am sure he made it up until the last few weeks of training before eloping with the barmaid. We had been told by our drill sergeant within the first few days of our training that this sort of thing happened on a regular basis and often with a barmaid from the Halfway House. The landlord of the pub was getting just a bit fed-up with the trainee airmen from Swinderby running away with his barmaids quicker than he could replace them.

People say you always remember the good times. Maybe it's my lack of ability to remember, or could it have been the brainwashing, but there is very little I remember about R.A.F. Swinderby.

I had now passed the R.A.F. basic training course – maybe that acceptance letter had come to the correct address after all. It was now time to move on to what we all thought was going to be the real Royal Air Force.

Caper Two

After basic training, it was off to trade training. Having selected Motor Transport Driver (M.T.D.) as my trade, I was off to sunny R.A.F. St. Athan. Many times I have heard that Wales is a lovely part of the world – well, not the part they call St. Athan. The locals, especially, did not like us and really didn't want us there. They didn't hide that fact, either.

Whenever we walked into a shop sporting a short haircut, we could hear locals speaking English until we arrived at the counter. Then they would change to Welsh. Then they would make you wait until, eventually, you got bored and butted in. They would then slate you for having bad manners. All I wanted was a packet of fags and they would make you wait just for devilment.

We also made their daughters pregnant – well, not me! But I remember some of the lads did. I had Tina at home and was happy to get drunk rather than chase girls. Mind you, you really wouldn't want to catch one of these girls. These girls were known as Valley commandos, from the Rhonda Valley. It seemed to me that all they were after was a clean-cut young airman to father their child. Even when the true father had finished his course and moved on, they would wait for the next batch of trainees and try to snare one of them.

Obviously, you cannot tar them all with the same brush, but they scared the hell out of me. These girls were as hard as nails. When they said dance, you'd dance. And when you went to the bar to buy them a drink, you'd run away; well, I did, and quickly.

When I got to St. Athan, our accommodation was no longer the 30-man room we had at Swinderby, but only 12. They had partitions that nearly made it look like real rooms; this, we told ourselves, was the real R.A.F. But we were wrong. There were plenty of airmen on-hand to remind us of that fact. This was my first time at St. Athan; I was here to get my basic car licence. I would have to return in three months or so to get my Heavy Goods Vehicle Licence (H.G.V.).

This is where I met Knuckles. He was given that name because, before he went out at night, he used to say, "I'm off down the bar. Anybody fancy a bit of knuckle?" (Did anybody want a fight?) He was quite a big lad, so very rarely challenged. Although he was a bit mouthy, I knew I could rely on him to watch my back. Shortly after I had met him, we were on our way to the Airmen's Mess for our dinner, when, from around the corner, came an Army captain. As I would normally, I saluted the officer and presumed Knuckles had done the same. He obviously hadn't and, as we passed him, there was a rather loud shout from the officer. "Airman, don't you salute Army officers in the Air Force?"

Knuckles grabbed my arm and very quietly said, "Leave it to me." He then answered the officer, "No, Sir."

The Army officer stood with a puzzled look on his face and said, "And, why not?"

Knuckles replied, "We haven't got any Army officers in the Air Force." He then grabbed my arm, dragged me 'round the corner and we ran.

As we ran away, we could just about hear the officer yell, "Okay, I'll let you get away with that one, but next time I'll be ready."

When you passed your driving test, you were put on a waiting list to find out where you were posted. I was given R.A.F. Wyton, in Cambridgeshire. I was lucky – I had aircraft on my station. Being new, we were told that you could join the Air Force and never see an aeroplane your whole career, which, I found out later, was possible. Some trades specialized in only one area and became limited to the amount of stations they could serve on. Fortunately, M.T. drivers could serve their time anywhere that had roads.

Once on the list, you could be hanging around for weeks and sometimes months. Finding something to do was always a problem. Fortunately, some of us had a little ingenuity. The brainwashing process from Swinderby had stopped working, or maybe was incomplete, but I managed to come up with a few ideas of my own.

The orderly sergeant came to clear the bar at half-past three every weekday. If you had any of your beer left and didn't have any afternoon work, you could stay as long as you liked to finish your drink. As soon as the sergeant left, we would get out small plastic beakers and push them through the railings on the bar. We would then fill the beakers from the pumps and pour the beer through the railings into our glasses. All we had to do was find somewhere to hide the beakers until our next afternoon off.

From 2:30, when the bar closed, until 6:30 when the bar re-opened, nine or 10 blokes can shift a lot of beer. Well, it gave us something to do in the afternoons, but of course it didn't take the bar staff long to work out that a lot of beer was going missing each day. So, we showed some other lads what we were doing, and before too long they were caught and we had to find something else to do on our afternoons off.

When I was at St. Athan, I had my 20th birthday. I never did much on my birthdays and I hadn't planned on doing anything that year, either. Knuckles, Sammy and Karl suggested a trip to Cardiff to break the boredom. Saturday morning, we got the bus into Cardiff and then straight into the pub opposite the Cardiff Arms Park. (It's not there now; it's the Millennium Stadium now.) We had been there several times before and, on a couple of occasions, were lucky to leave there alive. For some strange reason, their regular customers liked to sing, whereas we preferred to listen to the jukebox – really loud –louder than the Welsh can sing.

The pub was packed to the rafters. Everyone in the pub was having a drink before the big rugby match. The customers were four deep at the bar and, because we were not their favorite customers, getting served wasn't very easy.

At 1:00, the pub was almost empty again. We carried on having a laugh and joke at the expense of the Welsh bar staff, which was about normal for us. Then, without any warning, at about 1:30, the door opened and in walked Moss, Danny, Paul and Yjanic – all my mates from basic training. I just stood there like an idiot, completely dumbstruck. Karl said, "Come on in boys, and have a drink."

Up to that point, I was unaware that Paul's training camp was Weston-Super-Mare and that he had organized my birthday party – with the help of Karl – who was an M.T.D at Weston-Super-Mare, on his H.G.V. course at St. Athan. It is difficult to explain the relationship you have with someone who went through the hell of basic training with you, but there is a real bond-like friendship. Camaraderie seems so old-fashioned, but it's as close as you'll get to describe it.

The fact that we had Moss, a navigation instrument technician, and Danny, an air simulator technician, with four not-so-very-sober M.T drivers, showed we had definitely bridged the intellectual and class structural divide. We were about to have two days of what the R.A.F. referred to as high spirits, or what the locals called "a bloody disgrace."

Fortunately or unfortunately, I'm not quite sure which, I am unable to recall any of the events from that particular weekend. Maybe after speaking to a lawyer, I would remember some isolated incidents, although I am positive my birthday weekend would have been remembered by more than just a few airmen from R.A.F. St. Athan. If you ever visit the pub opposite the Millennium Stadium and you find "wanted" posters on the wall, of seven airmen, I wouldn't be surprised if one of them was of me.

St. Athan was not all fun and games. We were actually there to learn how to drive – not the easiest thing in the world to do, especially when you have been drinking copious amounts of alcohol the night before. St. Athan also had its own C.T. procedure – you couldn't just take as many tests as you liked until you eventually passed. Because of the R.A.F.'s lack of imagination, everybody was tied to "Three Strikes and You're Out." By failing my first test, I had put myself under a great deal of pressure; this is exactly what I didn't want to happen. There were both good and really bad examiners – all civilian – and, if you failed with a good, easygoing examiner, you were then given one of the not-so-good. Their only joy in life was to fail you on your driving test, but you didn't have to help them achieve that. With the help of too much merriment the night before, though, that was exactly what I did.

Out of all the examiners, the one with the worst reputation was a gentleman by the name of "Jumping Jim." As I had screwed up my first test, I, of course, was given "Jumping Jim" for my second attempt. "Jumping Jim" was a nickname given to him by the instructors (R.A.F. corporals) and then passed down to trainees and told by the instructors not to repeat it because the examiners was unaware of it. "Jumping Jim" was given the nickname because he was a very nervous passenger and, if while on test you were travelling too close to the vehicle in front of you, he would jump on the panic brake on his side of the vehicle. Because, and I quote: "The examiner had intervened whilst in the process of monitoring your driving test," this meant you had failed.

Before my second test, my instructor kept on and on, "Do not get too close to the car in front. Do not make the examiner nervous. Chew more chewing gum. And definitely do not call him 'Jumping Jim.' "

After all the stories I had heard, I was expecting a big old boy, meaner than a rattlesnake, when I actually ended up face-to-face with a nasty little runt with a Welsh accent. For the whole of the test he just barked out orders, and every now and again his right foot would twitch a little nearer to the panic brake pedal. At the end of the test and the usual road sign questions, he sat marking his clipboard, shaking his head. Eventually he looked up from the clipboard and said, "You haven't done anything wrong, but, to be brutally honest, I wouldn't let you push my wheelbarrow down the road." He then signed my form and slapped it into my chest. I said, "You're not here to pass an opinion. You're just here to sign my pass certificate."

As I walked round the corner, to my instructor and at the top of my voice, I shouted, "I only bloody passed and I had 'Jumping Jim.' " My instructor's face went from a very large, cheesy grin to a very embarrassed, red face. I hadn't realized, but the examiner was following me, probably so he could report me to my instructor for having a bad attitude. The examiner carried on, walking past me towards my instructor and said, "I now realize where your trainee gets his bad attitude from, Corporal." The corporal just smiled and said to me, "Congratulations, and thank you for the 'Jumping Jim.' It is about time someone told him."

I can't imagine that mine was the worst driving test that examiner had ever taken part in because the rumour doing the rounds was that a few years ago this particular examiner had to tell a driver, who was on his third strike, that he had failed. Unfortunately, he told the driver whilst still sitting next to him. The driver repaid his kindness by punching him in the face. Seemingly, that's how the instructors now know whether you have passed or not, because, if you have failed, the examiner shouts at you through the window after he has gotten out of the vehicle.

The examiners at St. Athan didn't exactly fill us full of confidence. While in our first weeks, a policeman who had only just passed his driving test smashed up an R.A.F. minivan. One night, on the airfield side of St. Athan and while on duty, he decided to have a bit of fun driving around the airfield. He had written a few doughnuts in the long grass and everything was going well, then he got stuck in a pothole at the side of one of the hangars. Instead of asking for help, he decided to move the vehicle on his own.

He'd worked it out that, if he rocked the van from side to side while the wheels were moving, the vehicle would drive out of the muddy pothole. His next problem was to keep the vehicle's drive wheels moving while he was on the outside rocking it. After a search, he found a breezeblock. He then lowered it onto the accelerator and while the front drive wheels were moving at great speed. He started rocking the van. Indeed, the wheels did manage to get some traction and the van drove itself at speed into a concrete pillar – part of the side of a hangar.

It would not be fair to completely blame an examiner, and you couldn't blame it on the talents of a corporal driving instructor. But, surely, someone during the process of teaching should have picked up on the lack of common sense on the part of this daft policeman and should have C.T.ed him long before he was considered for a driving licence pass certificate.

Caper Three

After St. Athan, I was off to Wyton. Now I was a real airman in the real Air Force. At last, a station that wasn't a training camp. With a new station, you always have to build a new set of friends. Unlike in the Army, airmen are posted individually, which means a new set of new friends with each posting. I think this is a good thing and, every now and again, you bump into mates you hadn't seen for a while. This gave you a good reason for a party, not that I ever needed a reason to party.

From what I can remember of Wyton, we used to finish work on Friday at 4:00 in the afternoon and didn't returned to the block (another name for a single man's accommodation, where most of the parties were held) until 5:00 Monday morning just to grab a clean uniform and shave before work. There were some fun times at R.A.F. Wyton, but even a simple game of football could be difficult if you'd too much to drink the night before.

Quarter to eight and I managed to crawl out of bed, surprisingly enough, considering the amount of beer we drank last night. I wondered if Sully and George managed such an achievement. I really couldn't see it, myself. Sully and George had been at Wyton for a year to 18 months before I had arrived and we had become good mates right from the start. Because Sully could never shut up, I once was thinking of re-naming him Lippy! But, bearing in mind his mate was called George, Lippy would probably have been translated to Zippy. That part of it I didn't mind, but, being the third member of the group, I just didn't fancy being called Bungle.

It was Saturday morning in early May at lovely, sunny R.A.F. Wyton, four miles from Huntingdon, Cambridgeshire, and we three lunatics were supposed to be playing football for the Motor Transport section (M.T). I had no idea who volunteered us for something so energetic, so early on a Saturday morning.

Kick-off, 10 hundred hours – that was how the R.A.F. said it – which is 10:00 in real money. I really did not feel well, but things had to be done. First on the agenda was to get the other two lunatics out of bed. Food, that's what I needed. And if I managed to keep it down, that would be a bonus.

Now for the fun part – waking those two up. Two jugs of water should do it. There you go – one for you and one for you. They were awake now, but both looked completely knackered; maybe Sully was just edging it, although I think it was unlikely that either could feel worse than I did.

George crawled from behind the sheet, which was supposed to be protecting him from his watery awakening (not that cotton sheets are waterproof), but, as they say, "any port in a storm." Please excuse the pun.

"How come you're up so bloody bright and early?" George asked.

"In case you hadn't noticed, it's nearly 8:00. We are playing football in two hours," I answered.

Sully then awakened from his watery grave. "I feel like crap," he said.

"I feel pretty rough, too," said George.

The night before, on the way back from the club, we had been separated. Sully and George then told me how they'd managed to break into the Airmen's Mess and found a leg of pork, which just happened to be lying around. After they had escaped from the Mess and consumed their spoils, they returned back to block at roughly four in the morning, some three hours after I had gone to bed.

"Well, it serves you right, you pair of wasters," I said. But they did look rough.

Nine o'clock and I was on my way to the mess for breakfast when the speaker system started bellowing out about a contaminated piece of meat that had gone missing from the Airmen's Mess and how dangerous it would be to eat the meat, and that whoever had should report to the Medical Centre for their own good.

I carried on to the Mess, thinking there was no way anybody would be daft enough to fall for that – not even Sully and George. After I had finished my breakfast, Pete came over to me and, through the giggles and smirks, said, "Have you heard that George and Sully went on sick parade?"

"No," I said. But maybe I should have known better than to leave those two to their own devices. I was on my way to the Medical Centre when my brain decided to kick in; well, to be truthful, it was when I saw the station warrant officer's car. There it was, sat right outside the Medical Centre with its own parking space marked S.W.O.

Years later, I would regard this man as one of the most positive influences to shape my young life. But, at that moment, he was looking for any excuse to have me locked up. He was under the delusion that I was some sort of ring-leader. What rot – I was five-foot, seven inches tall and 10 stone soaking wet. Who would listen to me? The fact that some brainless idiots did exactly whatever was suggested to them really had nothing to do with me.

Ten to 10 and everybody that was on the football pitch was running around in small circles. There were some trying to warm up and get the blood flowing, or they were stretching a muscle or two. Or, in my case, pumping blood through my alcohol stream without telling my head that it was day-time. If you can do this and resume drinking in a short space of time, it's possible to drink from Friday to Monday with only one hangover.

As I looked around the pitch, Sully and George were nowhere to be found. That was alright – they probably needed a good lie-down after their brush with death. Let's face it, eating dodgy meat can really take it out of you.

Peter and Sean walked over to me with somemore good news. Seemingly, Sully and George had owned up to pinching the meat, but, not content with two guilty parties, the S.W.O. had decided there must be a ringleader some-where in hiding.

Never mind, the game must go on. Ten to 15 minutes until half-time, and I had only been sick twice. But, this game was becoming seriously not fun. I picked myself up off the ground yet again and, as I got to my feet, looking through the sweat, mud and grass hanging from my forehead, I managed to spot the S.W.O. Maybe he was a football fan, standing on the touch line grinning at me.

After returning to the ground several more times, half-time was upon us – and time for my quarter of an orange. But my orange had been redirected elsewhere. I was then told I didn't need mine because I wasn't playing the second half. I'm not brilliant, but I didn't think things had got that bad.

The referee, who doubled as my section corporal, told me, "The S.W.O. would like a word." As I approached the S.W.O., I notice his broad grin.

"Yes, Sir, what can I do for you?" I asked. He went on to tell me that the leg of pork, which had been put aside for sandwiches for after the football match, had gone missing and that I knew the two lads that had confessed to doing it.

"Surely," I said, "You weren't going to give the footballers contaminated meat, were you Sir? Or were there two joints of meat that went missing last night?"

"You seem to know a lot about it," he said.

"Only what I've heard on the speaker system, Sir," I replied.

After a moment of silence and a pained expression on the S.W.O's face, he carried on. "How were you feeling this morning when you got out of bed? I hear you've been sick a couple of times during the first half." There was a shallow grin returning to the S.W.O's face.

"Oh, that was just nerves, Sir. I don't often get picked for the M.T. section."
And the grin was gone, shortly followed by the S.W.O. It was now time to find out what the story was with Sully and George.

It was 11:00 and the bar didn't open until 12. I was on

my way back to the block to try and get a lift downtown with Paul. Walking back into the block, I ran into George. "You Pratt!" I said, "Whatever made you decide to own up to nicking that joint of meat?"

"We were scared. We thought we had food poisoning."

"What do you think you're going to get for this?" I asked.

"The S.W.O. said if we told him who the third person was, he would go easy on us."

"Where did the S.W.O. get the idea there were three of you?"

He just stood there looking stupid, then said, "I think it was Sully."

After a long, boring inquest with the both of them, it turned out that they both said they couldn't remember due to the amount they had had to drink and, when asked, "And was Stewart there," they both said, "I'm not sure."

No wonder the S.W.O. was so interested in me. There had been a few incidents that had happened over the few months since I had arrived at Wyton M.T., and I had gotten away with a few misdemeanours, but nothing serious. It was all just high spirits.

In the end, Sully and George got 14 days' Jankers (for 14 days they had to report to the Guardroom after their normal day's work to be given pointless tasks for four hours for the soul purpose of keeping them out of the bar). I, on the other hand, was not implicated in this particular shambles, but I'm still regarded by the S.W.O. as the one that got away on several occasions.

On another occasion – again, some thought I should have been implicated – the Slightly Irritable Bawl (S.I.B.)

arrived at Wyton. As you've probably noticed, everyone in the R.A.F. talked in abbreviations, and it was difficult trying to remember what they stood for. For instance, there were not a lot of people who didn't know S.I.B. stood for Stupid Inept Bobby, or something like that (alright, S.I.B. stood for Special Investigations Branch, I think). But, if you met one, you'd never think that they would have the intelligence for it.

There were rumours flying all over camp that someone from M.T. had been caught nicking, and maybe I'd been helping him. What actually happened was the Motor Transport Officer (M.T.O.) had asked the Stunted Illiterate Bobby (S.I.B.) to investigate one of the M.T. Drivers who lived in a caravan across the road from the camp gates. And the Store Impounded Brain (S.I.B.) duly turned up on camp.

Anyway, they turned up at my mate, Alan's, caravan. Firstly, they couldn't find any of his neighbours to say a word against him and, secondly, they couldn't find anything that looked remotely stolen. So, they made an inventory. Sanctimonious Irritable Bore (S.I.B.) always made an inventory in case they forgot or didn't understand something that they could have a look at later.

Everything in the caravan was listed. There were several pages. Everything you could imagine was written down. At that particular time, Alan was on an economy drive and bought everything in bulk. Also, he could not afford a fridge or freezer.

A copy of the inventory report was given to the M.T.O. for him to have a look at. The day after he received it, he walked into the rest room with the report in his hand, his glasses on the bridge of his nose and looked down to where Alan was sitting. Alan looked up at him and said, "Is everything alright, Sir?"

The M.T.O. carried on looking, then said, "There are some very strange things in your caravan, Airman."

Alan just looked up and said, "Like what, Sir?"

The officer read from the list, "Are you aware that there are 32 pork chops in a plastic bag under your bed?"

Alan smiled and said, "Yes, Sir." The officer just stood motionless with a puzzled expression that bordered on complete confusion, waiting for an explanation...

"That's because I have eaten eight, Sir," replied Alan. (In the R.A.F. you always keep it simple.)

Caper Four

Six months later, I had to return to R.A.F. St. Athan for my Heavy Goods Vehicle Training (H.G.V.). This was normal and I quite liked the idea of running into the lads, who were due to return to St. Athan at the same time. I arrived two days later than Knuckles but it was the same set-up as before, only the right goby little tart that kept snitching on everyone had been replaced by a failed policeman who was there to get a license or be thrown out of the R.A.F. There were lots of times when we could, quite happily, have swapped the failed policeman for the goby little snitch.

Knuckles, I and the rest of the likely lads reverted back to our old ways and into our high sprits mode. The failed policeman became an even bigger pain than the goby snitch. Knuckles decided to take the failed policeman out for a drink and he readily joined us at the bar. I was beginning to believe Knuckles had lost the plot because he kept buying drink after drink. When I asked him about it, he just said, "Have faith. Watch and learn."

All through the evening, Knuckles sat with him and bought all his beer. Towards the end of the evening, I asked him, "Is there a point to this?"

He just replied the same as before, "Have faith. Watch and learn."

By the end of the evening, there was nothing left to do but for everybody to grab a corner and carry the drunken policeman home. Inside the block, Knuckles said, "Now we can do anything we like with him."

"Have you any suggestions," I asked.

"Actually, I do have one that springs to mind," Knuckles answered.

We all gave a hand and, before too long, the policeman was tied to his bed. His mattress and bedclothes had been removed and, with only his underwear on, he was lying on a rubber mat. We then left him for the night.

Around 6:00 in the morning, the lights in the block were switched on and everybody was woken up. I noticed there were now three electrical cables attached to the policeman's bed frame and a bucket of water in front of the bed – innovations that Knuckles had probably added during the night. I asked him, "What's next?"

Knuckles smiled, "We wake him up. It's education time, dear boy, education." We shook and shouted at the policeman until he was awakened from his drunken sleep. He started screaming and shouting about the predicament he had found himself in. Knuckles lifted up the bucket of water to show him. Eventually, he stopped. "What are you going to do with that?" he asked.

Knuckles explained to him that he was lying on a metal bed frame insulated only by a rubber mat, and that he had a bucket of water. The water, if thrown, would deem the rubber mat useless. The policeman sneered, "So what. Big deal. I'll get wet."

Knuckles smiled, "You don't seem to have noticed the electrical cables that are wired to your bed from the three-pin socket." That's when he started screaming again. The noise was deafening and, eventually, Knuckles managed to shut him up.

"If I let you go, are you going to behave yourself?" Knuckles asked.

The policeman just lay on his bed. The screaming had become just a whimper, and some of us felt sorry for him. Knuckles then said, "I don't believe you." He threw the bucket of water over him. The screams came back with a vengeance and with a rather large brown stain on his underwear.

All this education was to no avail, but our failed policeman was, indeed, very quiet for a whole week. The following Friday, Knuckles was going through his usual routine, "Anybody fancy a bit of knuckle?"

When our failed policeman couldn't resist calling him an idiot, Knuckles looked at me and said, "Some people just don't learn, do they?"

He walked over to the policeman's bed space. The policeman looked at him and said, "What are you going to do now?" Knuckles didn't answer; he just picked him up off his bed and threw him out the first floor window. I rushed to the window to see that he had managed to land on some bales of straw, which I never knew were there. I asked Knuckles later, "Did you know there were bales of hay there," to which he replied, "What do you reckon?"

I never did find out, but, knowing Knuckles as I do, I imagine that he had no idea that they were there.

The Air Force was good at keeping it simple – no

frills and you got what you were given. The Navy, on the other hand, was not quite so proficient. When I went back to Wyton, the Navy had run out of ships and had a few seamen left over without a ship. They decided to dish out the remainder to the rest of the services – the Army and the Air Force. At Wyton, we got Ted.

Ted had been in the Navy about four years and was what the Navy called multi-trade. He had three trades – air-traffic controller, fireman and driver. Unfortunately, Ted had only trained for two of his trades when they sent him to Wyton as a driver. The problem was, the only trade he hadn't been trained for was, indeed, driver. They had sent him to Wyton without a driving license, which is about as much good as a chocolate fireguard, but he did have a very good sense of humour. As soon as he arrived, you could see the corporals hadn't a clue what to do with him because he was only going to be with us for a short time. The corporals weren't sure what rank Ted was and would shy away from him. When asked, Ted would tell them he was the same rank as them, or higher than them, depending on how Ted felt.

As he had been travelling in a lot of hot countries, Ted wanted to keep up with his tan and managed to find some secluded places around the M.T. yard for sunbathing. One gorgeous September afternoon, a young lad, Martin, was taking out a three-ton lorry for a run. He had left the M.T. yard without a problem and was heading towards the main gate. As he turned a corner, he mounted the curb and drove into a lamppost. Martin said nothing to the bosses and, without saying a word, just took the blame and punishment for the accident. The bosses were unaware that Ted had crawled on top of the lorry and was sun-bathing on the tarpaulin canopy on the top of the vehicle. As he'd been up there for a while, he had dropped off to sleep and only awakened when he felt the vehicle moving. He then panicked and crawled to the front of the lorry, pulled himself over the front of the cab and, while looking through the front of the windscreen, screamed at Martin to "Stop!"

Martin, not knowing where he had come from, was screaming louder than Ted was. With Ted being in the way, Martin couldn't see where he was going and mounted the curb, then hit the lamppost, which torpedoed Ted off the front of the lorry and into a hedgerow. Martin couldn't say anything about Ted being on top of the vehicle because he had signed to say he'd checked the vehicle thoroughly before he had left the M.T. yard. So, he had taken the blame and was given seven days' Jankers for driving without due care and attention. Ted scrambled from the hedgerow, then took the next few days off sick and said he had fallen over when he was drunk the night before.

Ted and Ian, with a bloke from the Photography Dept. that none of us knew, and I decided to have an away day. Between us, we thought the Isle of Man sounded nice. Ian couldn't get time off at short notice, so I made a phone call and pretended to be his farther-in-law. I told the bosses that Ian's wife needed to get home to Scotland, as her mother was not well. Ian forgot to mention that our section sergeant lived on the same street as he and his wife. This was to become a problem for all of us, except for the bloke from the Photography Dept.

We arrived from the ferry onto the Isle of Man around 5:00 in the morning, in a not-so-highly-tuned Ford Escort Mexico that belonged to the bloke from the Photography

Dept. (I knew there had to be some reason for bringing him.) We then proceeded to have timed laps around the Isle of Man T.T. track in the not-so-highly-tuned Escort Mexico. No records were broken that day, but, if the locals had caught up with us, there possibly could have been a few necks. A sense of humour is not one of their best qualities at 5:00 in the morning.

After some breakfast, we set about getting drunk and looking for somewhere to stay for a few nights. This is where we struck it lucky. One of the first places that looked half-decent was run by an ex-policeman who loved listening to drunken servicemen. He would insist on serving us until four and five in the morning and his wife would come down in the early hours complaining to us for keeping her husband up so late. When she did come down, he would have to wake us all up and say to his wife, "I can't go to bed until our last customer has gone to bed. You know that."

We stayed on the Isle of Man for four days and a good time was had by all. The ex-policeman collected servicemens' headwear, so we left him with three R.A.F. berets and, of course, Ted's best Navy hat. He complained all the way home about how much it was going to cost him to replace his daft hat and that all we had to do was walk into clothing stores and ask for a new one.

It was when we returned to Wyton that our problems really started. Unbeknown to us, while we were away our section sergeant bumped into Ian's wife in the street. Of course, he, being concerned, asked her, "How is your mother? Is Ian back from Scotland? Why is Ian not at work?" Ian had told his wife that he had been sent to Cornwall and she was a little puzzled why the sergeant didn't know that. The sergeant then asked Ian's wife if she knew where I was. "Oh yes," she replied, "you sent him to Scotland."

Ian and I were summoned to the M.T. section for a chat. Ian was given seven days' Jankers. The sergeant and the M.T.O. were positive that it was me who had phoned to say Ian had to bring his wife home, as her mother wasn't well. Although it was never proven that I made the phone call, the R.A.F. had their own unique way of doing things and all charges against me were admonished. Admonished means you haven't done anything wrong, but, then again, you haven't done anything right. I was also given seven days' Jankers, just to stop Alan from getting lonely. None of the bosses even mentioned Ted being with us. I don't suppose most of them even knew he existed.

Ted only stayed with us for about three months, but we all got to know him pretty well and, when he left, we had a leaving party in his honour. While we were at the party, Ted mentioned to one or two of us that he wasn't sure which ship he was going to when he left Wyton and, if any mail turned up for him, could we keep hold of it and he would pick it up the next time he was passing Wyton.

About four days after Ted's party, a package turned up for him. The sergeant was going to post it on, but we told him, "Ted had said he was going to pick it up on his way through in a couple of days time." A couple of days went by and no Ted. The package, in the meantime, was getting a bit of a whiff to it. Eventually, the sergeant had enough and came into the tea room (where the mail was kept). He told me to open Ted's package, which, by this time, had a smell that was stomach-turning.

I took the package off the shelf and started unwrapping, with about three or four airmen and one sergeant watching me. When it was opened and the lid was removed, there inside was a rather large turd with a note in a plastic bag. It read, "Thank-you to all you shitheads at Wyton. I had a great time, hope to come and pay you all a visit soon. P.S. Don't go falling for any of those dodgy packages in the post!"

The Sergeant said he was going to have Ted reported. No sense of humour, these sergeants, but he didn't do any-thing about it and, unfortunately, we never heard from Ted again (I hope he is doing alright).

A few months later, we had a new driver arrive. Our section corporals pre-warned us about him, and they were not exaggerating. He'd had a few problems at his last sta-tion and had been given another chance with us because they knew we could put him back on the straight and narrow again (Well, it might have been.).

Daniel was a nice enough lad but had a problem joining in, so I took him under my wing; where's the harm in that? Unluckily, he didn't get off to a good start. His last station was a non-flying unit. Wyton was a new start for him and, under my expert guidance and tuition, he could expect to do well.

Tuesday evenings meant Late Crews – picking up the pilots from their aircraft (I hated it). It was a waste of good pub time. So Daniel, in an effort to get in with the in crowd, mainly me, offered to do my Late Crews. You can't blame me, it wasn't my fault. But he was embarrassed and, therefore, did not want to tell anybody that he hadn't driven on an air-field at night before.

On an airfield at night, it is impossible to tell the dif-ference between the road and surrounding area. You also

38

have to know what the different coloured lights mean and you have to rely on that experience. Even without experience, Daniel decided it couldn't be that hard, so he did not need any help or advice from anybody.

The first I heard of it was when George came into the pub and said, "Sergeant is looking for you."

"Why, what for?"

He explained, "You know that new lad that is doing your Late Crews?"

"Yes, what's happened?" I said.

"That's it! The sergeant wants to see you back at the M.T. section."

When I got back to the section, there were three airmen in the restroom. Not one of them said a word – they just pointed to the sergeant's office door. It wasn't as if I didn't know where the sergeant's office was.

I knocked on the solid door and a muffled "Come in" came from inside. I opened the door and walked in. Looking around, I was amazed at how many people you could get into that tiny little room. There was the M.T.O., sergeant, corporal, Daniel, a fireman, a policeman and an officer from the Airfield, who I didn't know.

The Sergeant was the first to speak. "Are you supposed to be on Late Crews, Airman?"

"No, Sergeant. I swapped," I replied.

The sergeant, now sneering, asked, "And you think it's alright to swap duties, do you Airman?"

I thought for a second, "Yes Sergeant, if you ask for permission first, Sergeant."

He put down the piece of paper he had been holding and, with a grin on his face, said, "And who did you ask for permission, Airman?"

Again, I thought for a second, watching the grin on his face disappear as he recalled the day's events, "If you remember, Sergeant...it was you and the corporal."

Neither said a word, and then the M.T.O. asked me to wait outside the office. After five minutes or so, the door opened. The M.T.O. walked out first, "See me at 9:00 in the morning, Airman."

"Yes, Sir," I said.

The rest filed past, with the sergeant bringing up the rear. He just snarled at me, "This isn't over yet."

"No, Sergeant," I replied.

As the incident was never mentioned to me again, it was over as far as I was concerned.

Myself and Daniel left the section at the same time. We had decided between us that the best thing to do after you've been dropped in the crap is to walk away and go for a drink. As we walked back to the pub, I told Daniel about the different coloured lights to be found on an Airfield and what they meant. Eventually, we walked into the pub together, when George met us at the door.

"Did Daniel tell you what he'd done?"

"No," I replied.

We both looked at Daniel. "Maybe we all should sit down," he said.

When we were sitting, Daniel continued, "These lights on the Airfield...I know about the blue ones, the green and the red ones on the ground. It's the triangular red ones and the white ones off the ground I didn't understand."

Myself and George started laughing, and then explained to Daniel, "The triangular red ones are normally found on the front of a towing tractor. And the white ones are to be found on the front of a towing tractor and, of course, on the wing tips of the aircraft being towed."

Daniel started to laugh and then explain, "I was driving down the runway surrounding area, when in front of me were the red triangular lights, the two headlights on the tractor and two high-up bright white lights on either side of the road. The tractor was in the middle of the road, so I drove 'round it. Without warning, my windscreen exploded, but it wasn't until I got out of the crew bus to see what had broken my windscreen that I realized there was a rather large aircraft behind me and I had just hit the underside of its wing." Daniel was given the mandatory 14 days' Jankers for that and a reminder of how precariously balanced his career in the Air Force had become. That was not to be the only disastrous bit of driving Daniel was to show us before he moved on to greener pastures.

On a cold December Friday night, the M.T. section was invited to the Rugby Club for a pre-Christmas party and everybody turned up. There were officers, sergeants, airmen and their wives and girlfriends – practically the whole of the M.T. section. After completing his 14 days' Jankers for trying to fit a rather large bus under a very small aircraft stunt, Daniel and his wife also attended.

Everybody seemed to be having a good time, even the officers were enjoying themselves. Surprisingly enough, most officers are good entertainment once they relax and have a drink.

The party was made up of lots of secluded little groups. Our group was made up of the usual lunatic suspects, on a table next to the single civilian girls. Sully had strategically positioned our table and theirs for the best position of attack. He had also declared himself the M.T. section's number one stud. This particular night we had put five pounds each under the ashtray on our table and played a game we called "Spot the Grot." It was harmless enough, if you weren't perceived as being the Grot. The rules were quite simple (which coincided with the airmen who played it). All you had to do was dance with a young girl, sit her down at your table and then introduce her to the rest of the table.

One or two of the lads had a go, then Sully started to dance with a young girl. She had not been at the front of the queue when they were giving out good looks. None of us had either, but it was our game. All the lads, whilst waving the five-pound notes at him, were shouting at Sully, "Don't bring her over. You've won!"

The girl then looked at Sully and said, "Are you playing Spot the Grot?"

Sully became embarrassed and said to the girl, "Yes, I'm sorry. But I didn't win."

To which the girl smiled, then replied, "I did."

The evening progressed as normal...the odd drunk telling a corporal what they really thought of him (not to be recommended), the odd wife bursting into tears and Daniel remembering not to drink too much (well, you can't have everything). By this time of the evening, Daniel was completely wasted, even though he'd been reminded of his rather shaky R.A.F. career.

Daniel decided to leave the party earlier than most. Not a bad thing, considering the state he was in. But Daniel never was good at asking for advice.

Fifteen minutes later, everybody had had enough and

it was time to go, including the M.T.O., as everybody started moving outside. We were greeted by the sight of Daniel on all fours, picking up bits of his number plate from out the side of the M.T.O.'s car. The M.T.O. looked down at Daniel and said, "Airman didn't you leave some 15 minutes ago?"

"Yes, Sir," replied Daniel.

"Then, surely, you could have made a good escape."

Daniel looked up at the M.T.O. and said, "Probably, Sir."

The M.T.O. turned to the sergeant, "Highly commendable, don't you think so, Sergeant?"

"Yes, Sir," said the sergeant.

"You could have driven away and no one would have been any the wiser," the M.T.O. carried on. "But, instead, you waited for me, to face the consequences." (One thing I learnt very early on in life is that, if you find yourself in the crap and someone is making excuses for you and even dragging you out of it, don't say a word. Let them.)

"Not exactly, Sir," Daniel butted in. And then, for some strange reason, Daniel explained, "I had had far too much to drink, Sir, so I told my wife to drive and, as she pulled out of the parking space, she hit the side of your car, Sir. I then jumped into the driver's seat and drove the car home. When I got the car home, I looked at the damage on my car and noticed my number plate was missing. So I brought the car back again to retrieve my number plate from the side of your car, Sir."

The M.T.O. stood looking at Daniel for quite a few seconds. Eventually, he said, "Airman, you have been very honest with me tonight and, with the exception of a bit of scratched paint and a bit of damaged bodywork, you haven't done a lot wrong."

The sergeant butted in, "Excuse me, Sir."

"Yes, what is it Sergeant?"

"I am not sure if you are aware, Sir, but the airman's wife does not have a driving license and has never had as much as a driving lesson in her life, Sir." After that startling revelation, the M.T.O. then changed his opinion on the evening's proceedings and Daniel was soon on his way to the job centre.

If you thought losing Daniel was in some way to eliminate the element of stupidity within airmen, you would be wrong. There was plenty to replace him.

Ian was just such an airman, and a good supply of entertainment as well. One Friday night, he had made a date with a girl from Huntingdon and had made arrangements to meet her in town. After work he ran back to the block and was washed, changed and into his good clothes. He'd ordered a taxi earlier in the day and that was waiting for him outside the block.

We all finished work at the same time and, by the time we got back to the block, Ian had gone. A few of us said it probably was his first date, but we were only joking. (I think it might have been.) Everybody went out for the night, as was usual on a Friday. Most of us went to the pub (no imagination, but it worked for me). It was the early hours in the morning when I, Sully, George and few others got back from the pub. I was just about to put my key in the door, when the door to the room next to mine opened. Paul, Ian's roommate, walked out into the hallway.

"Have you heard about Ian?" he asked.

"No. What's going on," I replied.

Paul then told the whole story of Ian's night out. When he had finished, he opened the door to his room and said, "Have a look at the mirror."

As I walked into the room, I was thinking about what Paul had told me! He said that Ian had had a long-term girlfriend before he had joined the R.A.F. She had finished with him when he left home to join up and he was very excited about meeting this new girl. Unfortunately, the girl didn't turn up. He waited two hours for her and then decided to get drunk. Meanwhile, a few R.A.F. lads saw him at the bar, drinking alone and knew why he was waiting there. They laughed at him and wound him up a bit before moving on. He then came back to camp and headed straight for the bar, where he got stuck into the drink somemore. By the time he left the bar and got back to the block, he felt pretty low and was steaming drunk. Having time on his hands and thinking about things too seriously, he thought it a good idea to jump out the window. His room was on the first floor, fortunately, and only about 12 foot from the ground. After jumping out the window, he landed in the rosebush directly below his window. He then scrambled back up the stairs and into his room. It was only then that he noticed the blood streaming from his behind, caused by the thorns from the rosebush.

It is drummed into you, very early on in your R.A.F. career, that you are not to ruin R.A.F. equipment. And getting blood on bed sheets is ruining R.A.F. equipment. To protect the sheets, Ian bared his bum to the mirror and stuck a full box of small round plasters to cover the cuts on his bottom. It was due to the amount of alcohol he had drunk, that I was now looking at a mirror covered in small round plasters. Ian was given seven days' Jankers for destroying R.A.F.

45

property. In time his confidence grew and, after a short time, became quite the Jack the lad, never again having a problem dating girls.

There was a process that Ian had to go through before he became that fully confident Jack the lad. He had to be completely humiliated first. He grabbed his opportunity by firstly changing to a new set of mates. After a drinking binge one night, they decided they wanted something to eat before retiring for the evening. They knew there was always food kept in the Airmen's Mess, so it was decided that was their main target. They determined the best way in was over the roof and through the oven air vents.

The initial assault went very well, and they were all loaded up with goodies and on their way to a victorious campaign. When Ian decided to fall through the roof, not only did he manage to destroy a large section of the roof, he also landed in the tropical bird aviary. And, when he fell into that, the birds flew out. His so-called mates left him there from two in the morning until the orderly sergeant opened the Mess at six in the morning. Ian had tried to get out, but, with the sides of the aviary being smooth glass and with nothing to hold onto, he remained there. He gave the orderly sergeant a good morning smile, who then left him in the glass aviary for around 20 minutes so the kitchen staff could have a good laugh at him. Ian was released, only to be re-imprisoned into the custody of the Guard Room for 14 days.

Ian returned to his former comrades (that would be us) after his 14-day holiday, wiser and well on the way to becoming yet another thorn in the side of the station warrant officer (S.W.O.).

It was at Wyton that I started to see another girl (I

must remember to finish with Tina). It's been 29 years since I met Janet (I'll get 'round to telling Tina one day). Janet was a local girl from Huntingdon; I met her at the nightclub on R.A.F. Wyton. She was sitting at the same table as Sully and his girlfriend, with her boyfriend.

I moved my chair between Sully and Janet, obviously knocking Janet's elbow once or twice so I could to start a conversation by apologizing to her. Steve, the airman Janet was sat with, didn't think it a great idea for me to be joining them and was talking about moving tables.

"By way of an apology, I'll buy the next round," I said, "and you can give me a hand, Steve." Steve and I then went to the bar and ordered a round of drinks, after Steve had paid for them. I explained to him there was no need for him to return to the table because I had found a tray and could carry the drinks myself. I then returned to the table with the tray of drinks and apologized for Steve's disappearance and his failing towards Janet. Then, I was only too happy to step into the breach and look after Janet for the rest of the evening.

Not being given the gift of the gab, Sully initiated most of the conversation and brought his own girlfriend more into the group, so as everybody could talk together. There's something else I must get around to doing – look up Sully (it's been a few years).

Sully was great to have around. He used to take the heat for all the things I didn't do, but the S.W.O. thought I had done. I remember, once, we were on exercise (that's when everybody runs around in the dead of night, pretending to be at war), and we had a new sergeant. It was his first exercise. We all got dragged into work at about 5:00 in the morning (same as usual) and he had been given the job of

47

signing everybody in. Five minutes after the alarm bells had rung, he was signing in the three musketeers (that would be me, Sully and George, just in case you hadn't worked that out).

The first question we were asked was, "What shift do you want to be on?" All three of us said, "Night shift, please, Sarge."

"Okay, three of you can stand down until shift changes 1900 hours." (That's the military time I was telling you about. That would be 7:00 in the evening.) So, it was back to the block and off to bed for us, so we could recoup our energies for the evening shift and war games. Yes, like that was likely to happen. Being Monday, what did actually happen was we were off to market day in St. Ives. On market day, the pubs were open all day.

We have had some great Mondays in St. Ives. But, we had to remember that we were on duty when we got back to camp. Firstly, off to the Mess for a late breakfast. You have to line your stomach before you go drinking on market day. Then jump on the bus to St. Ives.

At 10:00, we stood outside the pub waiting for it to open at 10:30. We were in a queue, which was made up exclusively of airmen from Wyton. Obviously, ours wasn't an original idea. Ten-thirty, doors opened and we were making our way to the bar – but not before we'd had the speech from the landlord. In it, he mentioned high spirits a lot. Although we were a fairly troublesome lot, most landlords liked it when Wyton had an exercise, as it was good for business.

I, Sully and George had a good day, and it was time to think about getting back to camp. We'd picked up another musketeer – his name was Scouse. Scouse was a driver, the same as us. Everybody else seemed to get on with him, but I found him a bit loud. As per normal, Scouse had managed to pick a fight, but not with one of the civvies as was usual. He had thrown down a challenge to the entire Wyton fire section from the entire M.T. section. The thing about firemen is that they are remarkably fit and, if one of them hits you, you tend to feel it.

To be honest, it was quite amusing with all those airmen knocking lumps out of each other. The few civvies that were there just stood watching. It was a strange situation and I think the civvies were jealous that they didn't have anyone to hit. Previously, the pep talk we'd had from the landlord did mention that he had gotten to the end of his tether and, if there was any trouble between the airmen and civvies, he would probably close the bar forever.

Technically, the bar should actually still be open. In the landlord's words, and I quote: "If there is any trouble between civvies and airmen, the bar will be closed." In actual fact, everybody who was fighting were airmen. So there you have it: Scouse started it, the landlord reneged on his original deal and yet the closing of that bar was still attributed to me. How unfair was that? Sully, though, made sure the blame was set squarely on Scouse's shoulders.

Word travelled fairly quickly back to Wyton and, of course, to the S.W.O. We arrived back sometime after five with the obligatory carry-out. Back at the block, drinking less beer and eating more solids (food), we set about getting back to a reasonable state of sober – something that definitely wasn't going to be possible within the next day or two (let alone, the next hour or two). After we had given up with that, Scouse had an idea. "Why don't we tell the bosses that we are drunk and can't drive? What can they do if we all stick together?"

I thought that sounded like a plan – not a great plan, but we'd had a lot to drink. Ten minutes to seven and we were on our way to work with the plan as we approached the section. We turned the corner and found there was a reception committee waiting for us, consisting of the new sergeant, flight sergeant and the M.T.O. All had that silly, fixed grin on their faces. They must have known about St. Ives and all the trouble, but they didn't mention it. No doubt we'd hear about it later.

"Good evening, gentlemen," said the M.T.O.

Then Scouse piped up, "We've had too much to drink, Sir! And we are not able to drive, Sir."

"You can go on perimeter fence fire watch," said the M.T.O. On that job, you have to stay out all night in the cold. "And, when you're not on duty, you can make tea for the rest of the lads."

Scouse looked up at the M.T.O. and very sheepishly said, "Yes, Sir."

The M.T.O. then looked directly at me and said, "How about you, Airman? Are you fit to drive?"

"Yes, Sir. Not a problem, Sir."

Sully and George followed suit and all three of us walked into the tearoom. When inside, one of our corporals, and a good mate, saw the state we were in so he rushed us to the other side of the airfield and put us on tanker duty. That was sitting in a chair, drinking coffee all night. Well it was, the way we did it. Later, the corporal said he didn't fancy doing all that paperwork from all the accidents we would have caused.

When we left the section on the way to tanker pool, we could see Scouse standing in the rain by the perimeter fence. To this day, I still have a little chuckle as I remember the expression on Scouse's face. He did hear about the trouble in St. Ives later, and was given 14 days on Jankers, along with two firemen. The S.W.O. was yet again disappointed not to see me swell the ranks on Jankers. Although there was a rumour that I was involved, nothing was ever proven.

With Scouse on his best behaviour due to doing his Jankers, I ended up having to clear up the mini-battle between the M.T. and fire sections. I asked the firemen to join us in beating up the photography interpreters, which we could have done easily by ourselves, but it makes the firemen feel useful. Besides, everybody knows it hurts when a fireman hits you.

Caper Five

All through my R.A.F. career, we had inspections and exercises. The inspections were hard work, but there was always a bit of fun to be had. I remember one year on the Air Officer Commanding inspections (A.O.C.s). The air officer commanding (A.O.C.) is an air commodore or higher rank (air commodore is only three ranks below Prince Philip), so, when you get one with a good sense of humour, you're doing well. Our A.O.C. had a great sense of humour and often sided with the men rather than the officers. As was usual, before A.O.C.s there was a pre-A.O.C. inspection. On the pre-A.O.C., the M.T.O. played the part of the A.O.C. and a sergeant played the part of the M.T.O. It was like a dry run, meant to make sure everybody knew what they were doing.

This particular sergeant was called Stan the Man. He was known as a bit of a practical joker and had a great sense of humour as well. Stan made sure everything was gleaming and spotless for the pre-inspection. As he and the M.T.O. headed towards the end of the inspection, they walked into the locker and toilet area. The floor had been painted red and then polished until it sparkled. The M.T.O. stood open-mouthed, looking at a large turd in the center of the floor, and, whilst pointing directly at it said, "Sergeant, what is that?"

The Sergeant walked forward, bent down on one knee and picked up the offending object. He put it in his mouth and bit the end off. "It is shit, Sir!" replied the Sergeant.

The M.T.O. scrambled from the room with his hand over his mouth and the sergeant in hot pursuit. Eventually, the sergeant managed to stop the M.T.O. and told him, "It's nothing but a prank, Sir." He explained to the M.T.O. that he had prepared it the night before and all it was, was mixed bread, milk and cocoa powder. After a giggle, the M.T.O. asked him to set it up again for him, for the oncoming A.O.C. inspection.

"The A.O.C. has a good sense of humour. He'll love it," said the M.T.O. So it was sorted.

The day of the inspection came, and the M.T.O. and the A.O.C. were nearing the end of the inspection. Then they came to the locker and toilet area. As was expected by the M.T.O., the turd was in place. "Sir, what the devil is that?" asked the A.O.C., pointing at the well-placed turd. The M.T.O. walked over to the offending turd, bent down and picked up the still-warm, 100 percent genuine turd and said, "Shit, Sir, shit. I'll kill that bloody sergeant!" To which the A.O.C. started laughing.

After a good 30 seconds, the A.O.C. had stopped laughing. He then said to the M.T.O., "Did you use Stan the Man for the pre-inspection?"

"Yes, Sir," replied the M.T.O.

The A.O.C grinned and said, "When you next see Stan, can you tell him from me he's getting a bit old-hat?"

"Sorry, Sir," said the M.T.O.

"He played the same prank three years ago to one of your predecessors and now he's at it again," said the A.O.C.

Exercises were a pain, but, looking back, we had some good times and some really good laughs. The format for all exercises was the same. Towards the end of an exercise, they would simulate the dropping of an atom bomb. That meant you had to wear your chemical suit and respirator, making it very difficult to work out who's actually underneath it.

One particular airman decided to confront his girl-friend whilst she was at work, with his chemical suit, respirator and with a rifle tucked under his arm. He walked into his girlfriend's place of work, pointed his rifle at her and said, "Put your hands up and give me all your money!"

With her not being able to recognize him, she pressed the alarm button as she had been trained to do. Did I forget to mention? She worked in the camps branch of Barclays bank. Well, all hell broke loose and there were officers and policemen running 'round like headless chickens. The Police were asking the junior officers whether it was part of the exercise and the junior officers, in turn, were asking their most senior officer, without alerting the station commander. Unfortunately, he did find out and, if I remember it right, that airman was given 28 days in jail and lost his girlfriend.

Although there were a lot of laughs on exercise, you really did work long hours. At the end of an exercise, you could use a good break, or party. We used R.A.F. Alconbury for rest and recuperation (RR – posh name for a party) on a regular basis. When we were there, we could use the Sergeants' Mess, and we would tell the Americans that S.A.C. stood for Senior Air Crew. It actually stood for Senior Air

Craftsman. The beer was half price, so it was worth telling a little lie to get in. Also, they used to have girls bussed in to Alconbury – some from Corby. Corby was my hometown before I joined the R.A.F.

If I found it difficult getting a taxi back to Wyton, I would get on the girls' bus to Corby and go see my mum, and, on the odd occasion, I might go and see Tina.

Whenever we arrived at Alconbury, the American police who patrolled the base made it really difficult for us to get on base. I don't think they liked us very much; maybe because we didn't like them either. Being young and easily excitable airmen as we were, and trying to impress all the young ladies, none of us said we were drivers, store men or, indeed, firemen because we were all pilots. The odd exception was Davie.

Davie had to be more. Besides being a pilot, he decided he also had a yacht and had asked a particular young lady to accompany him for a weekend's yachting. She, on the other hand, had had much less to drink than our Davie and didn't believe a word that passed his lips. She insisted on some form of proof.

Davie, being a Jack the lad from Stevenage, had persuaded her by giving her the proof she wanted – although he never told anybody else how he'd managed it. At the end of the night, on the way back to Wyton, he still insisted he had proven to this young lady that he did have a boat and the date was still on. Waking up on Saturday morning, there were hangovers everywhere – with the exception of Davie. He had a clear head and no hangover (don't you hate people like that), and no memory of the girl from last night, or, indeed, a weekend's yachting.

The rest of the weekend proceeded as was normal. It was then back to work on Monday morning. As soon as we all walked into the Tea Room, the sergeant told us, "There will be an I.D. (identification) check in five minutes. And all airmen are to produce their I.D. cards."

Davie couldn't find his, so had to run back to the block to look for it. He returned without it – just in time for the inspection to start.

The sergeant looked 'round the room, smiling at us. Then, with a large grin on his face, he said, "Okay, gentlemen, let's have a look at your I.D. cards."

As we all rummaged through our wallets, the sergeant stood watching Davie. (To lose your I.D. card is an offence punishable by prison.) Eventually, Davie said, "I seem to have mislaid mine, Sergeant."

The Sergeant then addressed everybody else in the room, still smiling. "It is an offense to lose your I.D. card, gentlemen." (See, I told you). Then he looked at Davie. "But it's just damn right stupid to give it away to a girl you hardly know, just so as you can take her out yachting. And in a yacht you haven't got."

Davie's face dropped as it all came flooding back. Seemingly, he had told the girl that the most precious thing he owned was his I.D. card and he could not lose it. So, he had given it to her as an assurance he would turn up for their date.

Still looking at Davie, the sergeant continued, "This time you were lucky. It just so happens that this particular little girl is R.A.F. Alconbury's station commander's daughter. And, luckily for you, she has returned it." Now smirking, the sergeant finished off with, "Oh, by the way, Airman, the station commander may be paying you a visit sometime today. He wants to find out your intentions towards his daughter. Don't forget to salute him."

The station commander never did turn up, but Davie was scared stupid all day and very lucky to get away with only seven days' Jankers. I remember Davie spent a lot of time on Jankers while he was at Wyton and, when he left, we hoped his replacement was as much fun as he had been.

Around this time, Billy was posted in to Wyton. Billy was Irish, but had spent the last eight years in Sheffield before he joined the R.A.F. He really had a very strange accent. He was a really nice lad, but seemed to have very little luck for an Irishman.

At this time, Wyton was notorious for splitting up married couples. Billy had only been with us around six months or so. Rumour control had raised its ugly head as soon as his wife had arrived at Wyton; the rumour was that she had been having an affair with some fireman. Very shortly after this, she went home to her mum and Billy decided it would be a good time to start drinking with a vengeance. He also made Jankers a new career.

With Billy living on his own, it had become too expensive for him to buy all his meals from the Mess, so he started cooking for himself at home. He was no Egan Rona, but, after a short time, he managed to cook good food whilst extremely drunk – no mean achievement. Until one night after a bellyful of beer, he fell asleep with the frying pan on the cooker. There wasn't a lot of damage, but there was a lot of smoke and the Fire Brigade were called out. The following morning, the chaplain paid him a visit. This was nothing unusual. The chaplain just wanted to have a chat, to make sure

Billy was alright. This chaplain, though, started his conversation whilst pointing at his badge of rank and saying, "I hate these badges of rank. They put such large barriers between us, with me being an officer and you being an airman."

The chaplain said to Billy, "Don't worry about these badges of rank on my shoulder. Please pretend they're not there."

Billy just looked back at him and said, "Yes, alright." They both then sat down and the chaplain carried on speaking. "I've heard you've been having some problems with your wife gone and I understand you're having a few problems at work as well."

Billy just shrugged his shoulders and said, "I'm fine."

The chaplain continued, "I was wondering if this was not so much an accident, but more of a cry for help."

Billy looked up at him, expecting him to be smiling. He wasn't. Billy said, "You're having a bloody laugh, aren't you?"

The chaplain sat back in his chair and with an angry, very straight face, said, "Airman, remember who you are talking to! I am an officer and don't forget that!"

Billy said, "Sorry, Sir, I was just trying to remove some of those barriers you mentioned, Sir."

Some officers seem to think they are above everything, but you can always get back at an officer with a little patience and if you bide your time. In one instance, a particular officer tried to upset Nick. Nick repaid that officer's kindness while making him look a Pratt at the same time.

Nick was only at Wyton for about three months. He didn't want to be there at all. He was coming to the end of his R.A.F. career and had worked out that he would finish his career in Germany while staying out there with his German girlfriend. The R.A.F. had other ideas; they brought him back to England for three months to finish his time at Wyton. The problem for Nick was that he would have to pay car tax on his nice new car, not to mention rather a lot of money to his estranged wife. He thought he would never have to bump into her ever again.

One day when Nick was driving a crew bus, just after new laws had been introduced concerning the distances you were allowed to approach an aircraft, he picked up a group of three officers who had returned from a long exercise in Norway. They had obviously not been made aware of the new laws. The more senior officer of the group, a squadron leader, walked over to where Nick had parked, leant in through the open window and said, "Consider yourself charged, Airman."

Nick sat there in complete bewilderment while the officer returned to offload a few things from his aircraft. He then returned to Nick and, again leaning through the open window, said, "Airman, never let me see you this close to one of my aircraft ever again." Then he returned to his aircraft.

Shortly after, the Customs officer drove up in his car. Nick could hear all three officers and the Customs officer talking. Nick just stayed in his vehicle, listening and making mental notes. The officers were saying to the Customs officer that they had gone a little over their agreed quota and talked of how much were they going to be penalized. It was all a bit of a laugh and a little bit of leg-pulling for the three officers. After the Customs officer finished writing out their bills and was walking back to his car, Nick waved him over to the crew bus. He enlightened the Customs officer by telling him the way things were done.

An airman cleaned the windscreen of the aircraft once it had landed. This was done with a cloth that they kept in a bucket. Before the Customs officer got to the aircraft, the airman removed the cloth from the bucket and the officers put their goodies in the empty bucket. Before the Customs officer arrived, the windscreen was cleaned and the cloth replaced over the goodies. Nick pointed this out to the Customs officer and then suggested that he took a look in the bucket.

As you can imagine, he was not best-pleased. The Customs officer returned to the senior officer and made him pay the duty on seven watches. He also confiscated them for trying to make him look stupid. The officer also lost out because he had to repay the other officers who had given him the money to buy the watches in the first place. It can be fun spoiling an officers day!

Around this time, I decided to get married. It seemed like a good idea at the time. Because it was the month of June, that meant no A.O.C. inspection for me, (sheer coincidence). Sully was going to be my best man. The only problem we seemed to have was the R.A.F. priest. Not to put too fine a point on it, but he was a nutcase. My wife-to-be and I went to see him three times and he was definitely getting worse each time we saw him. His main problem was that my future wife was Church of England. I, on the other hand, was Roman Catholic. According to the priest, that made for a "mixed marriage." I thought they all were – one man and one woman. The priest kept on about the best marriage ceremony he had ever done. The people getting married hadn't invited anybody, but all their relations turned up anyway and the bride's uncle played a mouth organ. It got to the stage that he did not want to marry us, so we moved on to a civilian priest in Huntingdon.

And so, on a warm and sunny June afternoon, I was joined in Holy matrimony to Janet. All the way through the service, I half expected this weird lunatic of a priest to run into the service to try and have it stopped. He wasn't invited and never turned up, but he did hear we had gotten married. He never acknowledged me when he saw me in the street after that, but, as they say, all's well that ends well.

It went really well. Sully was a complete wreck and could hardly stand because he was nervous. It was good fun watching him stutter through his speech, but that was just a bonus.

My mum and dad brought all my old mates from Corby. It was good to see them all, but, to be honest, we were all very different people. Being away for so long meant we had all changed. I think I had probably changed the most of all. My new mates hated my old mates and vice versa. When I thought about the old days before the R.A.F. and the way we were and the things we used to say and do, I realized it was me who had changed beyond recognition and understood how both parties felt. It was a pleasant enough reception, with never a dull moment and the odd battle here and there.

This meant it was now time I stopped going to Corby on the bus with the girls. I didn't stop going for nights out at Alconbury after all the exercises we had to go through – I still needed to get my share of R and R. Another reason for not going back to Corby was, I really didn't want to bump into Tina and I wouldn't have thought my new wife would think it a brilliant idea either.

Not long after the wedding, Sully decided it was time for him to move on and see the world. After all, that was why we all had joined the R.A.F. He had been a good mate and it was hard to see him go. That was a part of R.A.F. life that everybody had to get used to. There was always a silver lining...yet another party. We decided that Sully's going-away party would be at a real ale pub in Cambridge. We went in a convoy of five cars and all with nominated drivers (I wasn't one of the nominated). We had to be fairly responsible. After all, most of us were drivers for a living.

The landlord of the pub was ex-army and, according to him, he had seen it all before. When people said things like that to me, it was like a red rag to a bull. We notified the landlord that, "Some of our games can be a little risky."

"Not a problem. Like I said, I've seen it all before," he said.

We then asked him, "Was it alright to play freckles?"

Again, the same reply. I found a paper plate on the bar and, with a serviette, took them both to the toilet. On my return, I had the serviette covering the paper plate; it was obvious that there was something underneath it. The landlord approached the large round table we were all sitting at. He stood watching for a moment. Eventually, he said, "What is under there?"

With the exception of me, nobody 'round the table knew either. I lifted the serviette to reveal a freshly-produced turd. "You dirty sod!" he exclaimed.

"I thought you knew how to play freckles," I said.

The landlord, now pointing at the turd, said, "What are you expecting to do with that?"

"I told you, we're going to play freckles."

"And what the hell are freckles when it's at home?" asked the landlord.

I then explained the game. When we couldn't decide whose round it was, we got a turd on a plate. We then sat with our chins around the edge of a round table. One person, who is not involved, would splat the turd. Then we counted who had the most freckles. The one with the most bought the round of drinks.

I stood waiting for his reply with a rather large grin on my face. The expression on the faces of the rest of the lads was fairly funny, too. The landlord turned towards me, smiled and said, "You're having a laugh, aren't you?"

"Yes," I said, "but you should never say, 'I have seen it all before' to airmen when they are in a party mode." The Landlord laughed, but the relief on the lads' faces when they realized they didn't have to do it was even funnier. I have played some strange games in my time, but that one was made up on the spur of the moment, just for the landlord's benefit. No, that is one game I have never played.

Our stay at R.A.F. Wyton was coming to an end. Sully and George had moved on to Germany and there were new faces moving into the M.T. section. I, myself, had been given a posting to Germany, but not until I had the little matter of a court martial to deal with. Yes ,we all get court eventually.

When I was on a night out at R.A.F. Alconbury, I managed to get into a bit of trouble with an off-duty American policeman. I didn't do a lot wrong. The crux of the matter was that he said he had identified himself as a policeman before I hit him. I, on the other hand, maintained he was completely incoherent and abusive, and couldn't be understood before I hit him. The court martial found me guilty and I won a 28-day holiday. The court martial thought it might be fun for me to do my 28 days on R.A.F. Alconbury.

In stepped the S.W.O. I told you earlier, I was going to regard the S.W.O. as one of the most positive influences in my R.A.F. career. He thought the verdict was ridiculous and that the American policeman had played a larger part in proceedings than he had cared to mention. Also, there was no way of me serving my sentence at R.A.F. Alconbury. I thought he was just jealous because if he couldn't get me locked up in his guardroom. There was no way the Yanks were going to get me locked up in theirs.

To be honest, the S.W.O. was brilliant. Nobody was going to get to me unless they were prepared to go through him first, and that was not going to happen. The S.W.O. called in a few favours and, by ways of the old boy's act, managed to have my sentenced reduced. I later served out my 14-day sentence in a freshly painted guardroom at R.A.F. Wyton Detention Centre. I knew it was freshly painted because I painted it, and the S.W.O., while passing on a few choice words of wisdom, watched me paint every stroke. I was only released to get my gear together and move on to my next posting in Germany.

Before moving on, the S.W.O. and I had a sit-down and a good long chat. Well, the S.W.O. did most of the chatting and I did all of the listening. Then I was off to pastures new. I had been posted to R.A.F. Gutersloh...

Where the hell is Gutersloh?

Caper Six

A bold new beginning in Germany

Gutersloh is in West Germany. Well, that's what they used to call it. I had an argument with a sergeant at Wyton before I left and that was after I promised the S.W.O. I would be on my best behaviour and become career-oriented. It wasn't my fault. I hadn't been getting on with this sergeant since he had arrived on Wyton. I believe it's called a clash of personalities, although I can't remember him having one. Basically, he had decided that I didn't do anything he told me to do quickly enough, whereas I don't actually remember do-ing anything he told me to do quickly or not. He had a stutter and he had a pet-hate. It would drive him mad if anyone fin-ished his sentences for him. When I did it, I was just trying to be helpful. He was giving me the same chat as the S.W.O. had already given me and it became very easy to finish off his words for him simply because I had already heard them from the S.W.O.

After less than 10 minutes of this, he finally lost the plot and rushed me into his office, which was a port-a-cabin away from the section's main buildings. Whilst inside, he told me about his sergeant mates in Germany who wouldn't stand for the type of backchat that I had been giving him for the last year or so. I reminded him that we were alone, with no witnesses, and could he remove his hand from my jacket collar before I removed his teeth from his head.

"That's it, I've had enough," he said. "Let's go see the Fli-Fli-Flight."

"Flight sergeant," I helped out, adding, "There is no way I'm going to the flight sergeant's office with you – no way – but, please, do remember, if you're going to make a career out of roughing up airmen, make sure you've got witnesses. That way, you may just keep your teeth a little longer." A few days later I was on my way to Gutersloh and didn't have to deal with that horrible little man ever again.

It was a Saturday morning and I was dropping down through the clouds on final decent into R.A.F. Gutersloh. Gutersloh was to be my new home for the next three years. With my new career-minded attitude (induced to me by the S.W.O.), the opportunities could be endless. Maybe sergeant, no, well at least corporal. Keep it simple. This was to be my second chance (well, alright, it was to be another chance) to bring around what would end up as my brilliant and glittering R.A.F. career.

For the last few weeks I'd been talking to Sully and George on the phone. They had agreed to meet me on arrival at Gutersloh. George was stationed at Gutersloh, but Sully had driven up from R.A.F. Rhiendalin, approximately 150 miles west of Gutersloh. The idea was for them to show me the sites, get me settled in and keep me free of trouble to pursue my brilliant career.

As the aircraft touched down and came to a stand-still, I thought to myself, "That it was a nice gesture to have the emergency services surrounding us on landing. Maybe they knew I was on-board and it was their way of saying, welcome to your new home at R.A.F. Gutersloh." After clearing Customs, I met up with Sully and George, who instantly frog-marched me to transit accommodation. They explained to me why the emergency vehicles were there. Unbeknown to everybody on the aircraft, before landing, an "Aircraft Crash State Two" had been called on our aircraft. This was not as bad as it sounded – a "State Three" was when an aircraft was having problems that could hinder a safe landing. A "State One" was when you'd had problems, had a crash and had problems resulting from that crash. Basically, you were part of a hole in the ground. A "State Two" was when you'd had your crash (as in our situation – we'd had a bird strike whilst leaving Luton) and there could be problems resulting from that crash that may hinder a safe landing. I think you could say, as new starts go, this was what you may call an auspicious start to my R.A.F. career German revival.

My bags were placed on the top of an empty bed space in the transit block for new arrivals; hopefully, nobody else would be using it. Within minutes, the three of us were across the road to a pub opposite the camp gates. I was in my first German pub, having my first German beer and probably quite a few more.

Our conversation was all about what it would be like to see our first aircraft crash. Sully was wondering how hard it would be to change from an M.T. driver to an aircraft pilot – probably so he could fly his aircraft into the ground himself. In George's case, he was wondering what it would be like to be in an aircraft crash. I myself had been nominated as some kind of stuntman, but I had no intentions of becoming some sort of crash test dummy by being strapped into the front seat of an aircraft so that Sully, for no apparent reason, could fly into the ground at great speed.

After a few more beers and a bit more chat, you could sense the nervousness coming from the German people sat around our table. The more we drank, the dafter the conversation grew. I looked at the German faces around the bar and they were all listening to this ridiculous conversation between three heavily-drunken foreigners opposite an R.A.F. camp, talking about crashing aircraft into the ground at great speed. Before we were asked, I decided it was time to move on, and for me to see a bit more of my new home.

George had suggested going to Gutersloh main town centre, because you can watch porn movies in the middle of the day. As we walked out of the door, I had a little giggle to myself and I have now come to regard that day as my welcome to my new home, welcome to R.A.F. Gutersloh.

When we got to Gutersloh town centre, George was still trying to convince Sully and me that a porno movie was a good idea. "I really don't think trying to watch a film and at the same time trying to read subtitles is such a great form of entertainment," I said.

George replied, "You don't have any subtitles. You just have to listen to it in German and make it up as you go." He continued to whine, but, luckily enough, there weren't any films being shown. There was, on the other hand, a dodgy-looking character in a suit and bow tie shouting at the top of his lungs.

"Come see the best band in Britain," he said in broken English. I stopped him by asking him who he thought England's best band was. Eventually he answered, still in his broken English, "I think, maybe, Queen."

"You're saying for 20 marks (equivalent to five pounds English), I can go inside and I will see the pop group, Queen," I said.

"Maybe," he said. "Very big British band."

Sully paid for the three of us and, as we went inside, I said to he and George, "I can't imagine for a second we are going to get to see Queen for a fiver." Once inside, we sat down and waited for the show to start whilst speculating about what we were going to see. I thought, maybe at best, a film of a live performance. Sully thought some sort of German tribute band and George was still whining that we weren't watching porn.

We must've sat there a good 30 minutes, wondering if it was some sort of hoax or money-making con and, if it was, they'd definitely cashed in. The place was packed. I really wasn't too bothered; Queen was not one of my favourite bands. Eventually, a man came out onto the stage and, in perfect English, said, "Ladies and gentlemen, for your afternoon's entertainment...Genesis."

The three of us turned to look at each other. I sneered and said, "Yes, a fiver and you get to see Genesis. I don't think so." Then the curtains opened and we all just sat there gob-smacked. It was Genesis – the real Genesis. We were sat in a second-rate 200-seat cinema, with near 400 people completely gob-smacked, watching and listening to Genesis for a fiver. This was the first time I had ever seen a band live and Genesis was my number one favourite.

The band played for just over an hour, but they were

definitely worth every penny. After the concert, we went on a pub crawl around Gutersloh. The locals were not great lovers of the R.A.F., but then we'd had too much drink to care. Later in the evening we just jumped into a taxi and, without saying anything to the driver, sped off towards R.A.F. Gutersloh. I think maybe he was psychic or had a sixth sense. There were the three of us, all with short hair, drunk and couldn't speak German...well, maybe he wasn't that much of a genius after all.

It was about midnight when we got back to the transit block. All three of us grabbed the nearest bed and George, who had his own room somewhere on the camp, couldn't be bothered to go look for it. The next morning we thought it might be a good idea to go for dinner. We would have gone to breakfast, but we had missed that by a long way.

The problem I had was that I couldn't find my bags. After an hour of turning the block upside down, George said that I could get a wash at his place. As soon as we walked outside we noticed that where we had slept was not the transit block, but a training block. We were lucky it was a Sunday; on Mondays that building was filled with officers and airmen on training courses and was kept locked over the weekend. I don't remember breaking in, but I'm positive none of us had a key. On the way to dinner we dropped in to the transit block to check on my bags. They were perfectly safe and nobody had been anywhere near them.

While we were checking my bags, we also noticed that the training building was at the opposite end of the camp from the transit block. Maybe George was trying to get his own back for not being allowed to go and see a porno film, which he was still complaining about. To this day, I still have

71

no idea how we not only got into that block, but also how we got onto the camp. If we had come through the main gate, we would have had to walk past the transit block.

Sunday went the same way as Saturday. On reflection, the whole weekend wasn't what you could call a great beginning to my newly-restarted career. Before I had left Wyton, one of the lads had said to me, "Before I went to Germany I was fit, and because of the good lifestyle over there, I came back a wreck. You're a wreck before you go, you'll never make it back." Considering the state of my head after only two days of a three-year tour, maybe he had a point.

When you arrived at a new camp, they gave you what was called an arrivals card that you had to get signed by every department on camp. Sully returned to Rhiendalin and I, with George's help, set about arriving at R.A.F. Gutersloh. The main problem I had was that my new S.W.O. would only sign cards after 2:00 in the afternoon, and didn't like the smell of beer on your breath. This was three hours after the bar had been opened. By the time I fully arrived with my card filled in, I had been on camp for 10 days. When asked why it took so long, I just said it was a big camp. I found out later, mine was not a record. One airman took 17 days to arrive at Gutersloh.

For the first two months of an overseas posting, you were unaccompanied. Your wife had to stay in England until you got allocated married quarters. The things you had to suffer when you were in the R.A.F. Being single for up to two months was not one of them – that was more of a perk.

Being back in the block took a bit of getting used to. With all that sleep depravation and alcohol abuse, it was sometimes difficult to keep up. After a couple of days training, I was back in the swing of things. It wasn't hard when you gave it your full attention.

At every new camp you have to get new mates. George and I were still good mates, and we had this lad, Chris, who would hang around. Chris was alright, but we didn't want him around all the time. On one such occasion, George and I had decided to go to town early. Chris had been told the night before not to drink too much, as we were going to make a day of it in the German pub opposite the camp gates.

During the night, it snowed. I had never seen anything like it – the weather in Germany was similar to ours, but a lot more severe. Chris ignored the game plan and got completely wasted. The following morning, George and I were up at first sparrow's fart. Clambering through the snow became good fun. Then we started throwing a few snowballs at the store men who lived in the block next to us. Both us and the store men then decided it might be a good idea to throw a few snowballs at a few Germans. Where could we find a lot of Germans?

We ended up at 12 strong and in the middle of Gutersloh town. For a lot of years, R.A.F. lads had been having the odd spat with the local lads from Gutersloh and, with the S.W.O not knowing who I was, it could have been anybody's idea. After about 30 minutes, it started to look a little like we may have gone too far – we ended up with practically every lad in Gutersloh on the opposite side of the market square, throwing snowballs at us. After a short while, the police turned up. I was now thinking about who was on their way to jail and for how long. I could just see the headlines, "World War III is started due to international incident.

I was just about to turn and slip quickly away into

the snow when I noticed the German Police were backing towards us whilst throwing snowballs at the German lads. The police were a lot fitter than us and, after a while, all the R.A.F. lads got knackered and sloped away, leaving the police and locals to have their own little war. Later, some of the police and most of the locals turned up at the pub we were drinking in. We all sat down and had a good laugh. One of the policemen asked me if we ever had snowball fights with English policemen. I told him, yes, we regularly had battles with the English Police. I didn't tell him we called them riots.

By the time we had finished having a drink, it was getting dark and we still had to get home. The police asked a farmer to give us a lift on his tractor trailer, as he was passing the camp gates and it wouldn't be too far out of his way. He did give us a lift back to camp, but only because the police would have done him for something. I really don't think he wanted to.

Back on camp, we told the store men we would meet them in the bar after we had been back to block to get changed. As we walked into our corridor, we could see in the badly-lit hallway, a figure sat down on the floor with his back to the wall opposite Chris' room. When we were close-up, we noticed it was Chris. He was wet through and blue with the cold. He was also steaming drunk. When we woke him up, he told us about his day. "I was late getting up and I remembered you said you were going to the German pub opposite the camp gates. After having something to eat, that's where I went. When I couldn't find you, I decided to stay and have a drink and wait and see if you two turned up. An hour or so ago I got bored waiting for you and thought I might as well go home. It was then I noticed how drunk I was. I got across the road alright, but then my legs gave out and I had to walk back on my hands and knees through the snow. And now I'm absolutely freezing."

I asked him why he was sitting in the cold corridor and not in his warm room, had he lost his keys in the snow perhaps. He started crying and lifted up his hands. They were huge and blue with the cold. He said, "My room keys are in my pocket, but the snow has made my hands swollen and I can't get my hands in my pocket."

If we hadn't come back to the block, Chris would have probably stayed there all night. After letting him in and putting him into bed, we quickly washed and changed, then returned to the party with the store men.

The M.T. section at Gutersloh was split into three groups. I started off on Deployment and the others were Tanker Pool and Station M.T. I mostly hung around with George, Chris and the forth member of our group, Erick. They were all from Station M.T. The Deployment lads were alright, but one or two were just a little too crazy – even for me.

During the good weather in the summer months, Deployment would have section bar-b-cues on the airfield – the idea being you couldn't cause a lot of damage on an airfield. Sound thinking, until you enter the equation of your typical Deployment driver, such as Adrian.

While at one of our typical bar-b-cues (our last, to be more accurate), officers, sergeants, airmen and their wives were having a drink and getting stuck into the odd beef burger. Adrian decided to get somemore beer, then he jumped onto the tractor being used to ferry the sausages and beef burgers from the Mess to the bar-b-cue. The M.T.O.'s wife told Adrian, "You have had far too much to drink and, if you don't get off that tractor, I will tell my husband."

Adrian replied, "Don't worry about it, love. I'll have a word in his shell like myself."

We believe (but, then, we're not sure) that Adrian then tried to drive around the main tent (the one with the M.T.O. inside it). Unfortunately, the five-ton trailer he was dragging behind him seemed to have a mind of its own and completely demolished half the tent and the bar inside it, also bringing down the side of the tent the M.T.O. was in. MTOs normally have low or very little senses of humour. This one had none whatsoever and wanted Adrian charged with attempted murder. Although it could have been dangerous, it was funny watching the M.T.O. and all his cronies clambering to get out from under the tent. Adrian eventually got 28 days in jail and a heavy fine for driving whilst under the influence of alcohol and without due care and attention. (Maybe he should have gotten "driving within tent.")

Most of the driving jobs on Deployment were a little unusual – either an unusual vehicle or an unusual environment. One day, while on crash duties, the alarm sounded and, as per the drill, we all jumped into our allotted vehicles. Most time alarms turned out to be false. This time, we were given the information that there had been an aircraft crash. A Jaguar had come down in the woods just short of the R.A.F. Gutersloh runway. Nearly all your time on Deployment was spent training to do something you were never probably going to do. This was real. In convoy style, we all drove out of the main gates – one behind the other.

The first job I was given was to form a cordon around the crash site. This meant tieing some black and yellow tape 'round some posts and trees to make a ringed barrier. It bothered me that anyone could lift the tape and walk under the barrier. Normally, the cordon from an aircraft crash site was 200 metres and I had been asked to set it at 500 metres. This could only mean one thing – that the aircraft had been carrying a nuclear weapon. Now I was hoping it might become a false alarm. I didn't really feel all that comfortable.

Mac, my section corporal, walked over to me and said, "You know what 500 metres means, don't you?"

"Yes," I said.

He carried on, "Keep your eyes open. Seemingly, they can't find the pilot. He's probably running around still tied to his chute. If you see him, give us a shout. And make sure he is stopped, or stop him yourself."

"Yes, I know how dangerous it is," I replied. (Supposedly, pilots get disoriented after they have ejected from an aircraft and possibly could run under a bus, or they could be dragged in front of traffic by their parachute acting as a wind-filled sail.)

Nearly an hour later, Mac walked out from the tree line with his arm around the pilot. The pilot was bleeding from the mouth. My relief then turned up with some soup. "Have you seen the state of the pilot," he asked.

"I heard Mac punched him and he's bitten the end of his tongue off. If you can't stop them running, you have to rely on drastic measures," I said.

He smiled at me and said, "Mac told me more than an hour ago, 'If I manage to get that pilot on his own, I am going to punch him so hard, he'll be knocked out for a week.' "

"But, why," I said. "Mac was supposed to be going on leave before this all happened."

As Mac and the bleeding pilot walked past us, he smiled from ear to ear, winked at us and very quietly said, "Now I can go on leave."

That was the first time I had been to an aircraft crash site. Very shortly after that, I had my second. I had not been in Germany long and was beginning to think this might be a regular occurrence. An American A10 Thunderbolt had crashed in a farmer's field, about 30 miles from Gutersloh. The Americans had sent a recovery team, but they all had come from England and none of them had ever been to Germany. I was assigned to them as a driver, to take them back and forth to the crash site. There were three of them – one officer and two sergeants.

I, myself, didn't have the best of starts when I introduced myself with my first name and the three Americans introduced themselves with their second (it wasn't my fault). The first sergeant to talk to me said, "We don't bother addressing ourselves by our rank," adding, "My name's Frank," and then he shook my hand.

I, of course, replied, "My name is Malcolm." It was too late. The officer and the other sergeant then introduced themselves by their surnames. I realized Frank was the first sergeant's second name. I didn't know, but it is quite normal for Americans to call themselves by their surname. I decided to say nothing at that moment; it would be something I would rectify when I didn't feel so stupid.

After I had been taking them back and forth for 10 days and we had reached the completion of the job, it was decided by my bosses that the Americans could finish the job without anymore help from me. What was left of the aircraft had now been assembled together and was waiting to be transported away from the crash site. The route that we had been using daily was fine for the Jeep, but the aircraft remains were to be removed by a rather large lorry. By the time they had made out a route and worked out how to do the job, it was midday before they had set off. I had returned to my normal duties on Deployment and was unaware of any problems they may have been having.

At 4:00, I finished my day's work and, therefore, went off to the pub. Seven o'clock in the evening, the Americans decided it was time to ring Station M.T; they were lost and needed help. Normally, this would not be a problem. Unfortunately, the evening shift-on shift had no idea who the Americans were. Also, things were a little more confusing than usual because the Americans were asking for S.A.C. Malcolm, the airman who had been working with them for the last 10 days. Of course, there wasn't any airman on either Deployment or Station M.T. by that name and Deployment didn't have an evening shift to ask (maybe I should have rectified the mix-up with the names earlier). It was cleared up around 9:00, by which time I had had too much to drink and couldn't drive. The decision was made to chauffer me around the roads that we had covered over the last 10 days in a hope we may bump into them somewhere.

We did manage to find them around 11:00 in a pub, but they and their lorry driver had been there since around 8:00. My chauffer returned to Gutersloh with instructions that I would travel with the Americans in the morning (that was a good night). We returned to Gutersloh in the morning with no more controversy, although my M.T.O. was a little curious as to why an American Air Force officer would address me by my first name, whereas I addressed him by his second.

A month or so later, I changed from Deployment to Station M.T. That way, I could put in for the real cream jobs. At least on Station M.T., most of your driving was done on the road – in buses and cars – and not in bloody great lorries, in fields and forests.

One of the cream jobs was the school bus run. The fact that the kids' mothers used to travel with the kids to school was what made it such a cream job. There used to be some very lovely young mums on the bus, yet it was another job that was never entrusted to me (who could blame them). Erick, on the other hand, was regarded as very trustworthy, and this one run was one he had longed for since arriving at Gutersloh.

One morning, Erick came in to work bouncing around like a two-year-old. Someone had gone sick and he had been given the school bus run. According to him, he was going to do the job so well that they'd have to give him the job permanently. But, before that, he would have to go for a briefing. It wasn't his regular run so the bosses decided to show him on a map where he had to go.

Showing Erick the map had taken longer than they had originally intended and now he was late, so he ran down to the old lean-to garages where the buses were kept, dived into the driver's seat, started up the bus and then screeched out of the lean-to garage. Unfortunately, when driving out, he hadn't given himself enough room and the rear bumper of the bus caught the wooden centre post that was holding up the whole of the lean-to. There were witnesses who saw him turn 'round and watch in horror as all six bays of the lean-to collapsed like dominos, but still he carried on and finished the school run.

On Erick's return, there was quite a reception commit-tee waiting for him, which included the station commander, the M.T.O. and the station commander's driver. As Erick had brought down the garages, the station commander's driver was cleaning the station commander's car under the lean-to. The driver wasn't hurt, but the car was a complete write-off, despite the fact that the station commander had been allo-cated a brand new car. He didn't like it and still insisted on holding onto his beloved old car. Erick had now forced him to use the new one. This really didn't please the station com-mander at all.

Erick only got 14 days' Jankers. He had done well, considering the state the station commander got into over losing his pride and joy. Erick was never given the school run ever again and I never got to find out what it was like to even do one.

Shortly after arriving on Station M.T., Mac decided to join me. It was now fast-approaching Christmas. At Christ-mas and New Year, an R.A.F. station ran with a minimal staff. Normally, the single lads worked Christmas and the married lads worked New Year. I was doing that New Year because I was married, although I was also a Scotsman and Mac was too. (The officer who put Mac and I together obvi-ously had a sense of humour.) The officer in charge had man-aged to cheese off both of us. As by way of retaliation, you could say our hearts weren't in it.

After the bells at midnight rang, television became very boring. And ringing every relation and R.A.F. camp in England had become stale. We found it more fun ringing around other sections within Gutersloh, having a laugh with whoever was also on-duty. Mac ended up talking to an S.A.C.W. in the Air Traffic Control (A.T.C) and managed to get an invite for a drink. We thought about going down to have a drink, but, with emergency ambulance cover and the fact that we were the only ones in the section, it was best to say no.

As luck would have it, the section nerd turned up at about 2:00 in the morning to wish us Happy New Year and, being a complete nerd, he was sober. We asked him to do us a favour and watch the shop while we went to Air Traffic to wish them Happy New Year. Mac then rang the S.A.C.W. and told her we were on our way. Five minutes later, we were stood outside the tower, knocking on the door. A young lad S.A.C. answered. Mac asked him, "Where is the S.A.C.W. who wants sex?"

The S.A.C. smiled and said, "There aren't any S.A.C.W.s here. There's only me and the air traffic controller, and she is a flight lieutenant. Mac then said, "I've been talking to a S.A.C.W. all night. Just tell her Mac from Station M.T. is here."

At that moment, from behind the door, came an absolutely gorgeous flight lieutenant. Both me and Mac just stood there, gob-smacked. The flight lieutenant then came completely from behind the door and, while looking at the two of us, said, "It has been me you have been talking to."

Mac was the first one of us to react. "I beg your pardon, Ma'am."

I followed with, "Yes, me too, Ma'am."

She just stood there smiling. "Who is Mac and who is in charge of the Station M.T.?"

I pointed towards Mac and said, "This is Mac, Ma'am, and I'm on my way back to relieve my relief, Ma'am."

Five minutes later, I was back at Station M.T. I had sent the nerd home – he'd been asking too many questions. I was now pacing up and down the office, wondering what had happened to Mac. Thirty minutes after I had left him, into the office he walked with the largest smile you had ever seen. "There is no way you..."

Mac interrupted me, "I am not telling you anything. You wouldn't believe me."

To this day, I never did find out what happened to Mac for that 30 minutes, and I am still not sure if it had anything to do with any flight lieutenant air traffic controller (but I still remember that was some smile).

At Wyton, the married quarters were on camp, but the quarters in Germany were off-camp, set up like little towns isolated from the Germans. At Gutersloh, we were lucky to have the Germans right on our doorstep (this meant more parties). We lived in a small village called Hareswinkle, around six miles from R.A.F. Gutersloh in a group of flats called Lego Land, surrounded by private German housing.

When Prince Charles and Diana were married, all service personnel across Germany had their own street parties. Likewise, in Hareswinkle, we too had a street party, with a piece of bunting here and there and the odd Union Jack strewn across a few tables, and, of course, the standard 10 crates per man of your favourite beer. After an hour or so, two of our local German men approached us and asked if they could join our party, as they thought Diana was lovely and they wanted to celebrate the wedding. When we asked how many of them wanted to come, the German directly in front of me raised his finger and pointed in an arc-like fashion all the way around us. This indicated half the village. I said to him, "I'm not sure if we have enough beer, or space, for that matter."

The German looked across our communal car park and said that if everybody could move their cars into the surrounding streets, we could use that space. And, as for the beer, Germans always had enough beer.

The cars were moved and half the surrounding village moved into our car park with enough booze to float a small navy. There was the odd Brit who tried winding up the Germans with a bit of goose-stepping, but the Germans just ignored it. But they really loved it when some lunatic decided to dress up as Freddy Star's Hitler (yes, that was me). It was a great day and we all made lots of new friends, and the eating and drinking went on to the very early hours of the morning. I hope Charles and Diana appreciated the effort both the Brits and the Germans put in just for their wedding party.

Germans have a festival season, from September through until March, and, after that day of the street party, the Germans often invited us Brits to their festival parties. I would like to have said that I am still in contact with the German friends we all made over the three years I was at Gutersloh, but, unfortunately, that was a long time ago. Hopefully, some of the other Brits have still kept in contact.

Caper Seven

Prior to being posted to Germany, the wife and I were given a booklet and tape to teach us how to speak German. While at Wyton, we used to religiously practice our German, although we were not going to find out until later how useless this booklet and tape were to be.

On arrival in Germany, my wife and I had a lot of help from the R.A.F. and other airmens' wives. This is quite normal, and it would be our turn to help out with other new arrivals when they came to Gutersloh. It was understood that it was a different way of life to what most were used to. When you took over the keys to your quarter, everything was done for you. All you had to do was walk in through the door – even your shopping was done for you. After we moved in, I went to work and the wife explored our new village.

A lot of the time we used to eat in the pubs, and my wife met me after work in our local pub, called Hans' Bar. Hans' was made up of half English and half German. The beer was reasonable and the food was excellent. On one of the rare occasions when we stayed in, I noticed that we didn't have any food in the cupboard. My wife said she didn't fancy going to the shops because she was nervous speaking German. I told her we still had the booklet and tape, and she could give herself a refresher course before going shopping.

The next day, on my return from work, my wife told me she had been shopping and the cupboard was now full. Indeed, and so was the fridge. I said perhaps we should eat at home more often to save money. She just smiled. I started looking for something to eat when I noticed, in the fridge, one of the largest piles of luncheon meat I had ever seen. I said to the wife, "Why so much luncheon meat?"

She turned and looked at me, "That's why I didn't fancy shopping on my own."

I stood looking blank at her and said, "I don't understand."

She picked up the booklet and tape and said, "It's these useless bloody things." I decided to say nothing.

Two days later, we went shopping together. When we got to the meat counter, my wife smiled at me and said, "Carry on dear."

In my best German, I translated from the booklet, "Half-pound of luncheon meat, please."

The young girl behind the counter replied, "Sorry, I don't understand."

My wife smiled again, then told me, "It's in kilos, dear. Because I didn't know how much a kilo was, I said I'd have a kilo. That's why we have that large pile of luncheon meat in our fridge."

I was given luncheon meat sandwiches every day for two weeks, although I forgot to mention to the wife that, when I was at work, I had my lunch in the Airmens' Mess on camp.

It was only a short journey to work each morning and, with the tax-free car everybody had bought themselves, it was just as easy to drive yourself the six miles to work. Although there were a few driving laws peculiar to Germany, they were nothing you couldn't get used to if you concentrated. On the way to work one morning, when I wasn't concentrating as hard as should have been, I passed through a four-way junction. There were signs and traffic lights, all covered up, that were not there the day before. I really didn't take too much notice, but just carried on the rest of my journey to work as normal.

At the end of my day, I left work at 4:30 as was normal for my drive home (well, Hans' was actually my first port of call). As I drove along the main road towards the junction, that that morning had the covered-up traffic lights and signs, I realized I had just driven through the first of the speed restriction signs and I was now driving through a red light. Some two miles further on, I drove into Hareswinkle. As I slowed to the speed limit, I noticed a flashing blue light behind me. I pulled over to the curb and waited for the German policemen to get out of their car. As the two reached me, I rolled down my window. The smaller, but older, of the two, who obviously couldn't speak English, was jumping up and down, shouting what sounded like, "Hanging him." The tall, younger policeman bent down and spoke through the window, "You have annoyed my partner. Did you not see the road signs and traffic lights."

"YES," I said, "But, if we were in England, there would have been road works and road signs there for weeks before the road system would have been changed."

The young policeman smiled and said, "That is just

87

what the last English person we stopped said."

During this time, the older policeman was still jumping up and down, shouting, "Hanging him, hanging him." I started to explain to the younger one how dragged-out our road system changes can be. He raised his hand to stop my talking.

"The other gentleman we had stopped had already explained. Please, can you remember that, in Germany, our road works are completed in a lot less time than it takes in England. You can go now. Drive carefully."

As I looked in the rear-view mirror, I could see the argument flair between the two policemen and thought it best to get home as quick as I could.

I had only been at Gutersloh for a few months when I had my first exercise. (I was to be on several more while at Gutersloh.) I was in the block, having a kip, when Chris woke me and said there was a bloke in the bar who said he knew me. (During exercises, everybody is confined to camp or roaming 'round the woods looking for the pretend war.)

Chris said his name was Frances. I had no idea who Frances was, but I went down to the bar to investigate. As I walked through the door of the bar, I heard a string of abuse bellowing from across the room. I smiled and walked towards the noise. "So, your name's Frances, is it?" The bloke in front of me with the daft grin was Knuckles. He had been posted to the north of Germany and Gutersloh was a staging post. He was going to be with us for 10 days.

It was great having Knuckles stay with us; I was just a bit worried about how many times I was going to be charged, or even end up in jail, in the next 10 days. I had tried to visit him at his posting in London when I had been passing, but he was never around and his mates wouldn't tell me anything. He told me he had been in jail; he had been given 56 days for selling R.A.F. wheels and tyres without removing the service markings. He had come straight from jail to Germany for a new, cushy job driving around an air vice marshall up in the north of Germany.

Some blokes get all the good jobs. After a few beers and the odd scuffle (Knuckles was still offering a bit of knuckle to whoever might want it), we headed back to the block for some sleep. We both woke early next morning and decided to go for some breakfast. When I was ready, I knocked on Knuckles' door. He came out in his uniform. I looked at him and said, "You can get done for walking around with corporal tapes on your arm.

"But I am a corporal," he said. He went on to explain that, to drive around an air vice marshall, you had to be at least a corporal.

"But you just got out of jail," I said.

Seemingly, there was some lunatic officer at Knuckles' last London posting who'd had a chat with him. He told Knuckles that he didn't think Knuckles was a bad lad and, if he was given some responsibility, he would change his attitude accordingly. Knuckles just grinned at me, "This is the new, responsible me. What do you reckon? You'll see – for the next 10 days you won't recognize me." (with the exception of the string of boozy nights and the odd discretion with an airmen's wife and, of course, the odd rule being slightly bent due to high spirits) This was what Knuckles referred to as his first 10 days as a more responsible airman.

After the 10 days, there were pluses. I didn't spend any nights in jail, but only just managed to avoid Jankers by the skin of my teeth. And my wife was still married to me. Three weeks later, after the exercise had finished, Knuckles decided to come and visit for a weekend. He had a new girl-friend that he wanted us to meet. We had plenty of room at our flat in Lego Land, so he and his girlfriend could stay with us.

On the night, he was running a bit late so we told him we would meet them at the nightclub. The both of them turned up around 9:00; myself and the wife had been there for an hour or so and were well settled in.

When Knuckles and his new girlfriend arrived, I grabbed him by the arm and said, "Come on, I'll show you where the bar is." As we set off, Knuckles introduced his girl-friend to my wife and then we were off to the bar.

Myself and Knuckles returned from the bar with our drinks and, of course, a drink for the girls as well. My wife did her usual routine, "Where the hell have you been?"

"I've been at the bar talking to Knuckles." (I suppose she had a point, we had been away for nearly an hour).

"I have been sitting here on my own," she said.

"How have you been getting on with Catherine," I asked.

"That's what I mean. She doesn't want to talk to me. She's just ignoring me," my wife went on.

Knuckles came over. "How are the girls getting on," he asked.

I told him, "Seemingly, your girlfriend doesn't talk a lot."

Knuckles turned to my wife and said, "You are speak-ing in German, aren't you?"

"Hold on," I said. "When you left three weeks ago, you

couldn't speak a word of German."

Knuckles then smiled and said, "If that's the only language the girls speak, then that's the only one I have to learn."

And he had, in just three weeks, gone from not a word to practically fluent. He had done this just to get a girlfriend. (I bet he didn't use the tape and booklet me and the wife had used.) His girlfriend didn't speak a word of English and hadn't a clue what my wife was saying to her.

Knuckles and his girlfriend stayed for the rest of the weekend. Knuckles and I decided on the Saturday that the girls needed to get to know each other a bit better. So, we sacrificed quality time with our respective partners and had a boy's night out while the girls stayed in and had a good chat. With our usual resourcefulness and keen imagination in full flow, we both decided the pub was a safe bet. Not Hans' Bar... we went to the Wobblely Pub.

The Wobblely Pub got its name from the fact that it sold a beer called Warsteiner – a very, very strong Pilsner. When you'd had three or four pints of it, you could no longer pronounce Warsteiner, so you called it Wobblely because that's how it made you feel. At the end of the evening's enter-tainment, we were running around with a Rumtof jar on our heads proclaiming it to be the F.A. cup.

The Rumtof jar was an antique porcelain pot kept in a glass display cabinet. For some strange reason, they had unlocked the cabinet and had walked away and left it. I remember dancing around with it on my head, but I don't remember anybody taking it off me. I also remember, on the way home, saying to Knuckles, "Come and meet my mate."

On the way home, we had to pass a farmer's field.

When we got to it, we stopped and I pointed out into the darkness. "That's my mate." In the middle of the field there stood a large greyish-white horse. I had stopped and chatted, and then fed apples to the horse a few times before on my way home from the pub. As was normal, as soon as he had seen me, the horse started to walk towards the fence where we were standing, and, as usual, I fed him an apple from the side of the tree the horse couldn't reach.

We just stood talking to and stroking the horse after he'd finished the apple. Knuckles said, "Have you ever tried riding him?"

"No, "I can't ride a horse. I suppose you can." Knuckles smiled and said, "I thought everybody could ride a horse."

"Not me, and definitely not after the amount of drink I've had," I said. I'd had a lot to drink, but, the next thing I knew, Knuckles was on the front and I was on the back of that horse, walking round its paddock.

Knuckles said, "I take it the man with the shotgun is the farmer and you know him."

"Yes, I think that is the farmer, but all I know about him is that he is a miserable old sod."

Knuckles then said, "So it's possible this plank might shoot at us."

"Yes, I think he might. In fact, I'd bet on it."

Knuckles said, "Hold on," and turned the horse to-wards the opposite side of the paddock to where we had gotten on. I proceeded to fall off the horse, partly because of the bad horsemanship of Knuckles and partly due to the sound of the shotgun being fired into the air. Well, I hoped he was shooting into the air, in the belief that he wouldn't shoot directly at us...on the off chance that he might hit his own horse. I clear-headed, got to my feet and ran straight towards the horse, where Knuckles was dismounting onto the fence. (You would be amazed at how quickly you sober up when someone starts shooting at you.) I ran straight towards the horse, still hoping that the farmer wouldn't shoot his own horse.

The horse, by this time, was running around like a headless chicken. While running towards it and avoiding its hooves, I still managed to find a gap in the fence. We lay on the ground, giggling at the prospect that we could have been killed. Knuckles wanted to throw stones at the farmer in retaliation for his shooting at us. I decided that that was hardly a fair fight, that Knuckles had lost the plot and then I proceeded to drag him home. Before we got home, the nerves started to kick in and, by the time we got there, we were both shaking like leaves – and were sober.

As we walked into my living room and into the light, it was fairly obvious we had not just gotten home from a gentlemanly walk to the pub and back. My wife looked me up and down and, with that facial expression normally reserved for murderers and child beaters, said, "What have you two been up to?"

I looked at Knuckles and he looked at me, and the nerves disappeared only to be replaced by hysterical laughter as we both tried in vain to say, "Nothing. We haven't done anything."

Some 18 months later, evidence from that night would reappear and I was going to have to explain it.

After Charles and Diana's wedding street party, we were often asked to parties thrown by the Germans to celebrate numerous different occasions. Like most of the couples in the local area, we had been invited to a few festival parties all around Hareswinkle, then more when we made friends with our new neighbours, Alan and Sarah, who had just moved in.

We had been invited to one of these type parties. The Germans organizing the party had also invited Alan and Sarah. One thing you have to remember about Germans is that they are very plain-speaking and will restrict the amount of words they use. Also, their translation of English is not always fully understood by the English they are speaking to.

Alan had been posted into M.T. Deployment and then moved onto Station M.T. with me. We seemed to get along alright. When they got quarters next to us, the four of us became good friends and I took Alan down to Hans' Bar for a drink a few times (probably a few too many for Sarah's liking).

Come the day of the party, I told Alan we would meet him and Sarah at the party. Alan, being new to the area, didn't know where the party was so it was decided they would meet us at our house and we'd walk down together. This turned out to be one of Alan's better decisions.

Just before 7:00, we heard a knock at the door. I opened it and just stood there, motionless. The wife shouted to me, "Is that Sarah and Alan?"

To which I replied, "Yes it is." Alan stood in front of me, dressed as the mad hatter and Sarah was dressed as a big pink rabbit. I had on a suit and bow tie.

Alan looked me up and down and said, "What are you going as?"

I managed to blurt out, "Waiter. I am going as a waiter." Unfortunately, at the same time, my wife joined the conversation. She was wearing a very expensive evening gown. I again managed to blurt out, "I am a waiter and my wife is Lady Diana."

My wife proceeded to spoil everything by saying, "It's not a fancy dress party." She then explained to Alan and Sarah, "When a German says fancy dress, they mean they want you to dress fancy, posh."

I was so unlucky. Just on the wind-up alone, walking into that party with Alan and Sarah dressed like that could have been one of my finest moments. Because my wife had explained to them (she spoils all my fun), Alan and Sarah rushed home and changed before going to the party. I still told everybody at the party, and I am sure that, even to this day, 25 years later, there are still some Germans that would refer to Alan as the mad hatter.

After that, Alan developed a thick skin and carried on drinking at Hans' with me. Out of all the blokes in the crowd who drank at Hans', Alan was the only one who had to work alongside me on a regular basis (how lucky was he).

One of the others in our group was a little bloke called Rob. Rob was the most chauvinistic Pratt you were ever likely to meet, and very proud of it. One Friday evening, we were all sat in Hans' having a drink, as was our usual thing, and Rob was doing his usual thing, which was annoying the wives – including his own. With Alan and Sarah being new to our group, they probably had had no experience of this level of chauvinism, and Sarah, especially, was getting just a little bit annoyed with Rob.

Eventually, Sarah stood up and, at the top of her voice, shouted at Rob, "What makes you so much better than me?"

Rob stood up and walked 'round the table to where Sarah stood. She just stood there motionless, glaring at Rob as he walked around the table. When he got to Sarah, he grabbed her by the hand and said, "Come with me and I will show you what makes me so much better than you."

As he dragged her through the pub towards the men's toilets, Alan turned to me and asked, "Will Sarah be alright with him?"

With a smile, I said, "Yes, don't worry about it. He's done it before."

After a few minutes, Rob and Sarah emerged from the men's toilets. Sarah was a great deal redder than when she first went in, and Rob was grinning from ear to ear. Alan walked over to his wife and said, "Are you alright, love?"

Sarah replied with a snarl, "Where the hell were you when some strange lunatic was dragging me off to the men's toilets?"

They returned back to the table, sat down and had a drink with hardly a word between them – just the odd occasional glance in Rob's direction. Alan then plucked up enough courage to talk to Rob.

"What happened in the toilet," he asked.

Rob, still grinning, said, "Your wife will explain it, don't worry. It just shows how men are more superior to women."

Sarah turned to her husband to reply, "In the men's toilets, there is a skylight that goes around the top of the two external walls. Rob was kind enough to point out to me that he can pee through the open skylight, and he offered me the opportunity to do likewise. Seemingly, because I couldn't, that makes men more superior to woman."

It was always the same crowd. One of us would get invited somewhere and we all used to turn up. There was usually the 12 of us (all married couples). Most of the parties we went to were in one of our own flats, or in one of our cellars within Lego Land. One night after work, at Hans', when we were having our evening debrief (that's when we'd tell each other how our day had been) – basically just another excuse for a drink – I was talking to Tony and his wife and they suggested to my wife and I that we should come over to their flat one night the next week, as they were having a party.

During the following week, I asked our other friends what they were wearing, what time to be there, that sort of thing. I was a little surprised to find out that none of our other friends from the group had been invited, and didn't want to go even if they had been.

On the night of the party, I was still a little apprehensive and had told my wife to stay close to me because there was something really strange about this party. Except for the fact we didn't know anybody at the party, everything was just the same as all the other of Tony's parties that we had been to.

A couple drinks and a couple of introductions later, we both had started to settle into the party. Shortly after 9:00, an empty fruit bowl was placed on the coffee table in the centre of the room. Tony then stepped into the middle of the room, raised his glass in the air and said, "Ladies and gentlemen, if you could replenish your glasses at the bar, we can move on."

I looked straight at Tony and said, "I really hope this isn't what I think it is."

Tony said, "If all the gentlemen in the room could put their car keys in the fruit bowl, which is on the coffee table." I walked across the room to my wife (it's at this point that I have to tell you that my wife was and still is fairly naive), grabbed her arm and said, "I think it's time we should be moving on."

As she looked over my shoulder towards the fruit bowl, she replied, "Why don't you throw your keys in the bowl? You might get that Porsche you've always wanted."

On the way down to Hans' Bar, I tried to explain to my wife what sort of party we had just come from, but she wouldn't believe me. Not until she walked into the bar and saw the smiling faces of the rest of our group of friends did she realize that maybe Tony and his wife were a little more adventurous than we were.

Exercises and war games were quite a regular occurrence at Gutersloh, and we rarely heard when one of them was about to be called. There was once when we did. One of our group, Harry, worked in the main signals buildings and was forever passing messages from one station to another. He had gotten wind of an exercise team flying into Gutersloh late on a Sunday evening, and an evaluation team arriving in the early hours of Monday morning. This information went 'round Gutersloh like wildfire; practically everybody knew an exercise was on the way. Some airmen tried to get leave and clear off out the way, but most had to stay and wait for the exercise to start.

On Sunday nights, Hans' Bar was usually empty due to the fact that everybody normally had work on Monday morning. On this Sunday night, before the exercise had started Hans' was packed to the rafters with airmen and their wives and children. Everybody knew that, once the exercise started, it could be five weeks before families would see each other again.

Inside Hans', all the talk was about the pending exercise and what shift you thought you would be on. The chat went on until the early hours of Monday morning, and the children had been told they could have the Monday off from school. Everybody had their kit packed. We weren't going to get caught out this time, as we were normally.

Normally, the exercises were called around 7:30, 8:00 in the morning. It was now 2:00 in the morning and we were all thinking of getting something to eat and a couple of hour's kip. Then, out of the darkness, firstly you could hear the sirens, followed by the flashing lights of the mini-vans circling 'round and around Lego Land. The exercise had been called early; everybody was running around like headless chickens. We were all trying to do the same thing, to get a lift into work from someone who was sober. Most people I knew were rarely ever sober, and finding someone at 2:00 in the morning, in a pub, was proving to be impossible.

One of the senior officers from Gutersloh rang up Hans' Bar and gave permission for all airmen to drive into work if they couldn't get in any other way. The German police had stopped one or two drivers, but had been asked to turn a blind eye due to the fact that one day it could be the real thing.

The German police lined the routes from the married quarters to the main gate and, when we drove past them, we waved and shouted thank you to them. I don't think they were overly impressed with us.

When we got to the main gate at R.A.F. Gutersloh,

we were stopped by a large group of German people protesting about the noise made from our aircrafts' engines late at night. As I was still feeling quite merry from the evening's socializing in Hans' Bar, I decided they had a point and joined their ranks.

I was giving out flyers to the passing motorists for the noise abatement society, or some such people, when I got the impression someone was looking at me. After gradually slowing down from the chanting of Marxist songs and the bolshie's attitude towards the drivers who didn't slow down, I slowly turned around to be greeted with the smiling face of my station commander.

He took a long, lingering look at me and said, "If I thought you were a serving airman at this station, I'd have you court-martialled."

I replied in my best German, "Excuse me."

I felt a little ashamed about being caught, but Gutersloh, being quite a small station, I felt quite letdown that my own station commander didn't recognize me. Never mind, that was just someone else I had to remember to avoid for the next two years. That list grew on a daily basis, with the names on it becoming more and more influential each day.

At the start of an exercise, the mini-vans not only sounded the alert for the large married quarters like Lego Land, they also had to go to the smaller, more isolated quarters. At Gutersloh, there was a great number of hirings – some small blocks of flats, and even single houses or flats miles from anywhere. The mini-van drivers had to get out of their mini-vans and knock on the doors to these smaller hirings when on call-out duties. They had to carry a registry with them because the hirings would often change hands.

One of our sergeants was very keen on making sure these registries were kept up-to-date regularly. Nobody was very sure why, but there were rumours that he'd knocked on a German's door by mistake. This was one of his pet hates, but, then again, he did have rather a lot of pet hates.

After every exercise, this Sergeant Milton religiously gathered in all the registries and questioned the drivers as they handed them in. After a while, the drivers got bored with the intense questioning and just said, "No problems, Sergeant," or "Same as usual, Sergeant."

The sergeant was seeing a senior aircraft woman (S.A.C.W.). She was a driver and everybody knew about it, but nothing was said. Now and again, someone would get upset because she seemed to be getting more than her fair share of the good jobs. On this particular call-out, she was given the job of driving one of the mini-van alert vehicles and, of course, she was given the smallest route (lots of small hirings).

Around 2:30 in the morning, this young S.A.C.W. got out of her van and knocked on the door of one of the single hirings, only to be greeted by a very irate German man who promptly punched her on the nose. He then explained, in broken English, "I have lived here, in this house, for over 10 years and, still, you English bastards wake me up every time you have a bloody war game."

The S.A.C.W. drove back to Gutersloh holding a bloodied handkerchief over her nose. Most of the other drivers were already at work and had been assigned their jobs for the exercise by the time she arrived. I, of course, was late from handing out my noise abatement leaflets and, as was not unusual, I had turned up just a little behind schedule, but just in time to see the S.A.C.W. run into the arms of her sergeant lover. As she explained to him what had happened, it became quite clear that the same thing had happened to him some seven or eight years beforehand, when he was an S.A.C. and this was why he was always checking the registries. The R.A.F. police were called in to start an inquiry into the incident and an interested party, Sergeant Milton, went along with them.

When the German opened his front door to them, he took one look at Sergeant Milton and said in broken English, "Eight years ago, I smacked you and you said no more knocking on my fucking door. But you and your friends still keep knocking. Maybe I smack you again."

No action was taken against the German householder, and that house number was taken off the registry. But, I'm sure there are loads more of them still on that list, just waiting to be knocked on.

Caper Eight

The M.T. section often worked closely with the R.A.F. police. Sometimes this could be a problem, but, others times, it could work in your favour.

There was one night when they wanted to stop me for suspected drunk driving. It was no good, me driving away and trying to hide on the far side of the airfield, because they all knew my car. Likewise, it was no good me using a false name when caught because they knew my real name. But, me knowing that still didn't stop me trying. Where it did help was when one of my best mates (who just happened to be a policeman) turned to the arresting officer and said, "Clear off. Leave this one to me. I'll take care of this Pratt."

On the odd occasion that this sort of thing did work out to my benefit, it wasn't too high a price for everybody knowing I had a policeman as a mate. Sean was my police-man mate, and everybody should have had one. He got me out of trouble on more than one occasion.

Because of him having a lot of shift work, it was most-ly the weekends when we used to meet up down at Hans' Bar. I repaid his favours by getting him exceedingly drunk and keeping him out until the early hours of the morning – which is why his wife hated me more than any other person on the planet, including his mother. And she really despised her.

After a belly full of beer one Saturday night, which had rolled into very early Sunday morning, we decided it was time to watch Sean's new videotape – probably an educational film of some sort – but, more than likely, a pirated copy of some porn film with animals in it.

Five of us decided to return to Sean's to watch this masterpiece of a film. We all had our can of beer and bag of crisps each, and, of course, we all had the obligatory cushion on our laps. (It's not nice seeing how much your mates are enjoying this particular type of film.)

We watched no more than the first two minutes of the film when Sean's wife walked into the room and belted her husband around the head with a frying pan. She was only a small woman, but looking at the motionless Sean laying on the floor, we could tell she could pack a punch.

She then turned her attention to me. "You take that filth out of my house before I hit you as well." (If you're wondering what Sean's wife had against educational films, it wasn't that educational.)

I said, "It's not actually my tape."

She scanned the room and asked, "Well, whose is it?"

Nobody said anything, but pointed at the motionless figure on the floor.

"Right," she said (referring to Sean). "He knows I don't allow this rubbish in my house and I will hit him again when he wakes up."

By this time, she had removed the tape from the machine and handed it to me. While glaring at me, she said,

"You take this with you and if I ever see it in my house ever again, I'll know how it got here and who I am going to hit."

I didn't see Sean for a few days, but, when I did, he was supporting a rather large bandage around his head. After two weeks or so, his wife had allowed him to go back into Hans' for a drink with me. Although Sean asked for it, I never, ever gave him his videotape back. I wouldn't say I was scared of his wife, I'm just not that stupid.

A month or two later, both our wives became quite good friends – a little disconcerting considering his wife never could stand the sight of me. She often popped 'round my house just to have a cup of tea and a chat with my wife, in the evenings when she had nothing to do.

On one particular Thursday night, I had nothing to do and decided to stay in. Around 9:30, Sean's wife knocked on the door. This was my queue to shoot off down the pub, but there was an English film with German subtitles on German television. There was usually one a month and, if you were feeling slightly homesick, they were worth watching. So, I stayed in and watched while the girls chatted.

Sean was not the most faithful of husbands and often took out other women and sometimes had the occasional meal with them. I had watched my film and left the girls chatting; it was now fast approaching 11:00. I decided to join the conversation with, "And where is Sean tonight, then."

Sean's wife turned, looked straight through me and said, "Where he is every Thursday night."

I paused and waited for her to complete the rest of the explanation. She then rejoined her conversation with my wife and I sat there waiting, with a vacant look on my face. Eventually, she turned to me again, smiled and said, "He's out having a drink and a game of darts with you – you know, the same as you do every Thursday night."

I had no idea what to say. I didn't have to say anything. She just smiled again and said, "Funny, but your wife tells me you hate darts with a passion."

That night, I stayed out in the pouring rain until two in the morning, just so Sean could change his alibi; it was all to no avail. Shortly after that night, his wife went home to England and I heard they were divorced soon after.

Once a year, we all went on a brewery trip where they showed us how beer was made. I went on three of these trips, but, unfortunately, I still haven't a clue how it's made. Sean's replacement for our group (although he wasn't a policeman) was Harry. Harry was Nigerian, with a great sense of humour and up for anything. He and his wife had just moved into quarters when one of these trips had been organized. The entire male population of the pub used to go on these trips and then split into two groups – of English and German – when we arrived at the brewery. We went by coach, with the aisles full of bottled beer for the trip. Everybody was usually half cut by the time we got there. (You'll have to try to imagine what we were like on the way back. I could never remember.)

When we first arrived at the brewery, the German half was given instructions and a timetable, and then sent on a three-hour tour around the factory. When it was our turn, we just said, "Don't speak German. Where can we get a drink?" We were then shepherded to the main reception area and told we could eat and drink as much as we liked. By the time the Germans had finished their trip, we were also finished (completely out of it). The coach was magically filled with beer and we were on our way home, still drinking.

We had told Harry it was only a couple of hours'
journey, but it was 8:00 at night and it had been 8:00 in the
morning when we'd first started. He decided to run home,
but had a small bladder and, with all the drinking he had
done, was ready for a good pee by the time he had got back to
the flats. Worse to come was when he thought he would save
time by unbuttoning his fly – one more problem was when
he realized he didn't have his door keys. So, when he came
out of the lift with his trousers around his knees, he had to
knock on the door and wait for his wife to open it.

At that point, Harry's plans quickly took a nosedive.
He got off at the right floor and knocked on the right door
number, but, when the door was opened, a young girl started
screaming at the sight of a drunken Nigerian with his trousers around his knees and his penis in his hand. It was during this screaming that Harry came to realize that, being a
relative newcomer to Lego Land, it was hard to differentiate
between one block of flats and another.

Things started to settle down after the brewery trip
until one morning when four M.T. drivers were called into
the M.T.O.'s office. With me being one of them, I was trying
to think what I had been caught for this time. But, looking
at the other three with me, I couldn't imagine any of them
doing anything wrong. They weren't exactly what you would
call my usual playmate type.

It turned out that some nit had invaded the Falkland
Isles and we four had been attached to the R.A.F. regiment
to go and get them back. We were quickly bundled 'round
to the squadron leader of the regiment, who pointed out
that he didn't like us and didn't want us getting in the way

of his fully-trained men. He felt that as his men were better trained, and being in a war situation, it was likely they would be watching over us rather than concentrating on their own safety. (He had a point, I suppose.)

It was at this time that the R.A.F. decided to reintroduce Basic Fitness Testing (B.F.T.). The idea behind B.F.T. was to make sure all airmen were as fit as they should be for their age. The three lads with me all had good running times on their B.F.T.s. Myself, on the other hand, had managed to find a loophole. The idea was that everybody had to run one and a half miles, although it depended upon your age as to how many minutes you had to complete it in. I had managed to swing it with the help of one of the medical secretaries to get hold of an escape chit (doctor's note), on account of my dodgy knee. I also had managed to keep it off my medical documents, which meant I had no B.F.T. deficiencies — therefore, A1 and good to go.

Anyway, we got to write our letters (the ones that start: If you are reading this, something terrible most have gone wrong). Then we were off. First stop, England. One of the funniest parts of that trip was the fact that there were 120 men, all with guns. We were on our way to war and hiding our guns all the way through Holland because the Dutch government wouldn't give us permission to travel with live firearms.

When we got to the ferry port in Belgium, all the vehicles in our convoy took up most of the ferry, with only a few civilian lorries and drivers allowed on with us.

As soon as we were on our way, everybody converged on the bar, including the civvies. (I think someone had told them that when they were with us they had become a military target, too.) The squadron leader didn't like the idea of anybody enjoying themselves, so he shut the bar, which meant the civvies couldn't get a drink either. One of our lads went to see the purser and managed to buy five trays of Tenants lager; we sat and drank all night. We also supplied the civvies with the odd tray of lager so they didn't feel left out.

We had been told we were on the way to Felixstowe, and that nobody knew what our movements were. But we were told by the civilian drivers that we were on our way to Dover and, if they didn't land there, there would be hell to pay. I'd finished drinking at 6:30, had a quick kip, grabbed a shower to sober up and was getting stuck into my breakfast. Then the loudspeaker system squawked out, "Welcome to Dover, the local time is 7:30." The time difference was only an hour, which meant I was still drinking less than two hours ago.

As we drove off the ferry, Customs officers shouted at me, "You're in England now, son. We drive on the other side of the road."

I replied, "As soon as I am sober, I will be right over there." The police officer in charge of our escort didn't look too chuffed.

We had been told that nobody knew we were in England, and nobody knew what our movements were except for the civilian lorry drivers, Customs officers, the police escorts, and the press and television people...and the thousands of flag-waving children that lined the streets on our 100- mile journey to Portsmouth.

While we were at Portsmouth, all the military accommodation had gone and we had to put up with a three-star hotel for two weeks. We were given £23.95p a day to pay for our meals and, while we were making good money, we were in no hurry to leave.

All the regiment lads were billeted on the QE2, but it was still undecided between Gutersloh and the squadron leader whether we were going to go with them or not, or whether or not our B.F.T. reports could be believed. It was a very nice break, just sitting around drinking all day, waiting for the bosses to make a decision.

Eventually, we were given our orders to leave our vehicles with the regiment and return to Gutersloh by public transport. Of course, we rushed back as quickly as we possibly could (public transport is very slow when there is a war on).

Eventually, we did arrive back at Gutersloh. Things had remained much the same as they were when we left. One exception was that Alan had become a more regular drinker and card player, and was now regularly being asked most weekends to leave the bar. I moulded back into the group, taking my place at the card table. We played cards every Sunday between 12:00 and 3:00...ish. After cards, we went home for Sunday dinner. Unfortunately three-ish became closer to four and even five. All the wives started to get a little cheesed off; Alan's wife, Sarah, obviously didn't have as good a sense of humour as the rest of the wives.

One Sunday, cards had run on until 4:00 – nothing unusual, but, this time, Sarah served up Alan's dinner and brought it into the pub. She sat it down in front of him on the card table, then very neatly placed his knife and fork either side. She said, "If you are going to stay here all day, you might as well have your dinner here."

Alan became embarrassed and felt he had to say

something, so he replied with, "You silly cow, you've forgotten the salt."

She then lent forward, picked up his plate and poured his dinner over his head. He stood up and head-butted her, which really rocked her to her boot. Then Alan walked from behind the table to help her outside. She wiped the water from her eyes and caught him with a right hook, perfectly on the chin, and knocked him out. She then stepped over him and sat in his seat.

"Is there anybody here who can show me how to play this stupid game?" She just sat there happily smiling to herself, as the men rushed 'round to help her choose a card, and every so often somebody would step over Alan.

After the Falklands war finished, we were told the regiment was on its way back to Gutersloh and there would be a grand parade for our returning heroes. All of the regiment returned to Gutersloh after the war, completely unscathed, although they did mention that they got really bored with Compo rations (dehydrated food sealed in plastic bags that the military gave you to eat in wartime). They did manage to supplement their rations by shooting one or two sheep on the island, which the Falkland islanders, in turn, became very quickly bored with. There was a great deal of alcohol drunk, both on Gutersloh at the arrivals' party and back at Hans' with family, friends and mates who managed to get out of going. I felt as though I was cheated out of what I had been trained for, although it was a blessing my wife never received that letter. There was some really embarrassing rubbish in that. I also missed out on one of the sweatshirts that the Regiment lads were wearing on their return to Gutersloh. The sweatshirt had a picture of a British Bulldog with a Union Jack draped across its back and with an Argentine flag hanging from its mouth. Written around it was, "The Empire Strikes Back." Unfortunately, the station commander thought them to be in bad taste and they were ordered to be destroyed.

Germany was good and I had a great time most of the time, but there was the odd fly in the ointment every now and again. One particular fly was when I bumped into my old stuttering ser-ser-ser-sergeant from Wyton who informed me that he had been posted to Gutersloh, just to set the record straight. I still had 12 months of my tour left to do at Gutersloh; I knew that working with this idiot was going to be difficult. Soon after he had arrived, the horrible little man made it quite clear that he hadn't forgotten our conversation from Wyton. He took every opportunity he could to ruin my day. At first, it was just something I had to put up with, but it very soon became boring.

We had some building work being done and lost our changing rooms. We had to put up with a temporary locker area outside the main offices. Everybody was aware that you could be seen by people entering and leaving the main office. One day, while I was in the locker area, I unzipped my fly to tuck my shirt into my trousers. A female sergeant saw me and said, "Airman, isn't there somewhere else where you could do that?"

I just smiled at her and said, "It's alright, Sergeant. You can't see anything. I keep them in a bag."

She just smiled and kept on walking. Fifteen minutes later, I was summoned to the flight sergeant's office. The female sergeant had come to visit my stuttering sergeant and he, in turn, had convinced her to try and have me charged with sexual harassment. The charges were dropped, but the situation had become silly. I then decided it was time to have another chat with my stuttering sergeant.

I was a little annoyed and probably not thinking too straight when the stuttering sergeant called me into the temporary locker area. I had a good look around before I entered the area, but couldn't see anyone as I walked in between the locker opening. The sergeant backed himself into a corner. I approached him and, by putting my arm around the back of his head, stopped him from backing in between two of the lockers. I heard a shout and looked up to see the flight sergeant smiling down at the both of us. He was shouting, "I'll be your witness, Sergeant."

I think this was the point where my bold new beginning started to look just a little bit shaky, so I replied, "Witness this," and then punched him. (I never have said I was intelligent.) Two months earlier, my wife had told me that we were expecting our first child. I had told her that this could be a chance for me to knuckle down and go for corporal, sergeant or one of those other endless opportunities there were at Gutersloh.

As usual, I had managed to screw things up again, or, as George Formby would say, "Turn out nice again." Over the next few months, my wife got larger and my court martial grew nearer. My wife's parents came to stay and look after their daughter as she got nearer the birth. I was put in charge of clearing a room for the in-laws to sleep in.

Our spare room was normally used as a dumping ground for all sorts of junk, and I was no longer surprised in what was found buried in there. Making the spare room a bit more inhabitable meant I had to move around a lot of furniture and uncover a mixed array of long-lost treasures. One such treasure was a Rumtof Jar that I had inadvertently removed from the Wobblely Pub and now had to explain to my wife what it was and where it had came from.

I remembered the night of the F.A. Cup celebrations and the horse-riding lessons with Knuckles afterwards, but I had no idea how I managed to get a valuable antique home in one piece, especially considering the state I was in that night. I told my wife that I had bought it from a bloke in a pub, but she also had been to the Wobblely Pub and had spent hours admiring those Rumtof jars in their display cabinet. I said that I would return the jar to the pub and wouldn't even think about attempting to take it through Customs on our return to England. (You'd be amazed at what you can get through Customs.)

The in-laws came and went without a hitch and proved to be quite helpful, but, because my daughter was a bit reluctant to be born, they had to return to England before her birth. One week later, after my in-laws had returned to England, it was the turn of my parents to arrive in Germany. They were immediately put on baby watch duty.

I had taken a week's holiday to spend some time with my parents and to join in on the baby watch duties. Most of the time was spent ferrying around my heavily-pregnant wife and conducting tours for my parents to see the sights in and around Germany.

On one particular day, my dad said he didn't fancy anymore traipsing around Germany and could use the time to catch up on his sleep. With that settled, myself, my wife and mother were off to see the local sights in and around

Hareswinkle. As I told you, it was quite rare to know when an exercise was about to be called. As it would happen (on my day off), that would be the day.

We were enjoying a gentle stroll, traipsing (as my dad would call it) around Hareswinkle, when we stopped for a beer. No sooner had the beer touched my lips that I heard the stomach-churning howling of the mini-van sirens. My first concern was that I would have to go into work. My wife's first concern was, "Your dad is in the flat on his own."

My mum chipped in with, "He didn't panic in the Second World War, there's no reason why he should now."

As we made our way back to the flat as quickly as we could, I was instantly made aware that there was no quick way of conveying a heavily-pregnant woman. When we did get back to the flat, we found my dad running around like a man possessed. As I walked through the door, he immediately announced, "I think World War III has just started."

Luckily for me, it was only a three-day mini-exercise and I managed to return home before my parents were due to return to England. My daughter had still not been born and my father still hadn't stopped shaking from his World War III experience. My parents returned to England and I returned to my unaccompanied baby watch.

The night before my court martial, my wife decided it was time to go into labour and she needed to be taken to the hospital. By the time I got her sorted and into the hospital, I was late for my own court martial. When I returned to Gutersloh, the R.A.F. police on camp arrested me. They thought that I had done a runner.

My court martial finally finished late afternoon, at 10 past five, although I had been a father since 10 to five. I still was given 56 days in jail for hitting the sergeant. Only fair, I suppose. You shouldn't go walking around hitting sergeants. Where would it end (although I still maintain he did deserve it)?

If you receive 56 days in jail when you are serving in Germany, normally you are sent home to Colchester. But, because my wife and daughter remained in the hospital for nearly a week after the birth, it was decided I could serve my time in Germany. The M.T. Section was very good and quite regularly supplied transport for my wife to come and see me in jail.

I met some good mates while in jail and one or two really strange ones. Haggerty was, by far, the strangest. He was one of four from R.A.F. Larghbrook and had been given 56 days detention for drug abuse. While we were at Bruggen, Princess Anne paid us a visit and we, as prisoners, were given the job of erecting the safety barriers. When you were in Bruggen Prison, you weren't allowed to have anything in your pockets – no personal items at all. All was going well with the barriers when Haggerty suddenly dropped to his knees, then to all fours, pretending he was a cow and chewing the grass. The corporal staff in charge of us shouted at Haggerty to get up. He just ignored the corporal and carried on mooing and shouting, "There is magic everywhere."

Being a druggy, he knew what magic mushrooms looked like and they were everywhere. The more he ate, the more stoned he got, and the corporal had no idea what he was doing. Haggerty just kept on going, occasionally lifting his head and shouting, "I've dropped my money," or "I've lost my watch."

The corporal replied, "You shouldn't have anything in

your pockets to drop." By the time the corporal got him to his feet, Haggerty'd had his fill and was stoned out of his head. The corporal was going to charge him for sneaking drugs into the prison, but the other corporals in charge of us told him what Haggerty was doing. The other corporals also thought it funny that the corporal didn't know what he was doing. And then, because the corporal didn't want to look stupid, he dropped all charges against Haggerty who got away with it scot-free.

When I returned to Gutersloh after completing my sentence, I had only a few months left before my return posting to England. Due to the 56-day holiday I had received, I was offered to return to England as a civilian. This doesn't mean I was thrown out of the R.A.F., although it was a very close-run thing. What it did mean was that, even if I had been a brilliant airman for the next 20 years, I still wouldn't be eligible for promotion.

The time I spent in the R.A.F. was, by far, the best days of my life and I would recommend joining to anyone. I possibly would do some things slightly differently, but, in the main, no regrets and, yes, I probably would have still been asked to leave the R.A.F. early. My once potentially brilliant and glittering career in the Royal Air Force was now looking decidedly dull and distinctly over.

I took up the R.A.F. offer to return to England as a civilian and received, by far, my biggest promotion since having joined the Royal Air Force. Before entering the Air Force, I was referred to as a youth (there were others names, but I would rather not be reminded). I had now re-entered civilian life as a "mister," and this was, indeed, what I am referring to as my biggest promotion.

I often think back to my days in the Royal Air Force with great affection and very fond memories. I think to myself, maybe, just maybe, with a little less high spirits and one or two more chances, things could have ended differently for me. Corporal, sergeant, flight sergeant, maybe even warrant officer. No, perhaps not – let's keep it real. After 25 years, I'm still married and now with three grown-up children. I think I am making a better mister than I ever did an airman, even if I do say so myself.

When I do occasionally think back to the good old days, it does cross my mind – What if my dad was right and, by some fluke of nature, the acceptance letter I got was really meant for somebody else?

If you were rejected admission into the Royal Air Force early in 1977 and I was inadvertently given your place, I do apologize on behalf of the R.A.F. for their mistake, but wouldn't change things for the world.

Note: *If you've read this and felt you've missed out, maybe you blame me for the misuse of your service career. But, remember the old adage, "It's what you make it." I'm afraid there is no guarantee that you would have had half as much fun as I did.*

The End.

Printed in the United Kingdom
by Lightning Source UK Ltd.
134277UK00001B/391/P